On the Runway Series

# CATWALK

YA $10.00 5|19|18

MARION CARNEGIE LIBRARY
206 SOUTH MARKET
MARION, IL 62959

*Other books by Melody Carlson:*

## ON THE RUNWAY SERIES

*Premiere* (Book One)
*Catwalk* (Book Two)
*Rendezvous* (Book Three)
*Spotlight* (Book Four)
*Glamour* (Book Five)
*Ciao* (Book Six)

## CARTER HOUSE GIRLS SERIES

*Mixed Bags* (Book One)
*Stealing Bradford* (Book Two)
*Homecoming Queen* (Book Three)
*Viva Vermont!* (Book Four)
*Lost in Las Vegas* (Book Five)
*New York Debut* (Book Six)
*Spring Breakdown* (Book Seven)
*Last Dance* (Book Eight)

## BOOKS FOR TEENS

The Secret Life of Samantha McGregor series
Diary of a Teenage Girl series
TrueColors series
Notes from a Spinning Planet series
Degrees series
*Piercing Proverbs*
By Design series

## WOMEN'S FICTION

*These Boots Weren't Made for Walking*
*On This Day*
*An Irish Christmas*
*The Christmas Bus*
*Crystal Lies*
*Finding Alice*
*Three Days*

# CATWALK
## ON THE RUNWAY

BESTSELLING AUTHOR
## Melody Carlson

BOOK TWO

ZONDERVAN®

ZONDERVAN

*Catwalk*
Copyright © 2010 by Melody Carlson

This title is also available as a Zondervan ebook.
Visit www.zondervan.com/ebooks.

Requests for information should be addressed to:
Zondervan, 3900 *Sparks Dr. SE, Grand Rapids, Michigan* 49546

This edition: ISBN 978-0-310-74810-6

Library of Congress Cataloging-in-Publication Data

Carlson, Melody.
  Catwalk / Melody Carlson.
      p.   cm. — (On the Runway ; bk. 2)
      Summary: When the Forrester sisters take their hit television show to
  New York for Fashion Week, they find that success in the big city comes
  with big challenges.
      ISBN 978-0-310-71787-4 (softcover)
      [1. Reality television programs—Fiction. 2. Television—Production and
  direction—Fiction. 3. Fashion—Fiction. 4. Sisters—Fiction. 5. Christian
  life—Fiction. 6. New York (N.Y.)—Fiction.] I. Title.
  PZ7.C216637Cat 2010
  [Fic]—dc22                                               2010008121

All Scripture quotations, unless otherwise indicated, are taken from The Holy
Bible, *New International Version*®, *NIV*®. Copyright © 1973, 1978, 1984, 2011 by
Biblica, Inc.® Used by permission. All rights reserved worldwide.

Any Internet addresses (websites, blogs, etc.) and telephone numbers in this
book are offered as a resource. They are not intended in any way to be or imply
an endorsement by Zondervan, nor does Zondervan vouch for the content of
these sites and numbers for the life of this book.

All rights reserved. No part of this publication may be reproduced, stored in a
retrieval system, or transmitted in any form or by any means — electronic, mechan-
ical, photocopy, recording, or any other — except for brief quotations in printed
reviews, without the prior permission of the publisher.

Cover design: *Jeff Gifford*
Cover photo: *Dan Davis Photography*
Interior design & composition: *Patrice Sheridan, Carlos Eluterio Estrada &*
*Tina Henderson*

Printed in the United States of America

15  16  17  18  19  20  /QG/  18  17  16  15  14  13  12  11  10  9  8  7  6  5  4  3  2  1

# CATWALK

# Chapter

## 1

*"Now, this is what I'm talking about!"*
I point to the building as Paige and I get out of her car. The entire front of this three-story boxlike structure is covered in a massive collage (made with recycled soda cans) depicting what I think must be a rhinoceros, standing beneath some palm trees and a colorful rainbow. "Seriously." I squint up at the shiny image. "How cool is that?"

"Right ... and if that's considered art, I can only imagine what the inside will look like." Paige shakes her head as we approach the old building. "I cannot believe Helen put this one on the list."

Unlike my sister, I know exactly why this design studio's on the list. And I'm glad for it. I've had it up to my eyeballs with all the slick uptown studios, those overly serious designers and their stick-thin models. I cannot wait to meet this particular designer. Because Granada Ruez is a *real* person—and she designs for *real* women. I've been a fan of her environmentally conscious clothing for several years now.

Last week, when Granada won an international design

award for humanitarian efforts in Third World countries, I brought it to our producer's attention. Paige may not know it, but I'm the reason we're here today. I'm the one who convinced Helen Hudson that *On the Runway* needed to feature Granada Greenwear on our local designers episode.

"This feels like a mistake," Paige says as she opens the door.

"Granada Greenwear may not be considered high fashion," I tell my sister as we enter the showroom, "but we need to give her a chance." I'm trying to contain my enthusiasm because I know it will only aggravate Paige. She's already dragging her heels.

As if to emphasize the fact that she's not into recycled clothing, Paige dressed to the nines this morning—and she's wearing a designer who recently made fashion headlines for his blatant disregard of certain environmental issues. "But his style is superb and his clothes are perfectly timeless," Paige told me after I pointed out her faux pas. She is so out of touch.

"We're here to see Granada Ruez," I tell the salesgirl inside. "I'm Erin Forrester and—"

"I'm Paige Forrester from *On the Runway*." Paige holds out her business card, taking over as if being here was all her idea in the first place.

"Oh, right." The girl peers curiously at us. "Hey, didn't I see you two on *Malibu Beach*—the breakup episode?"

"Yes, but that's not our show." Paige points to the card. "We're *On the Runway*. Have you seen it?"

"Not yet."

"Well, maybe you'll want to tune in ... in case we decide to include today's interview." Paige's smile fades from bright to tolerant now. And I give her a look that says *just be nice!*

"In that case, I'll be sure to watch it," the girl says.

"Our director and production crew should be here shortly," Paige informs her. "In the meantime, do you mind if we look around your shop and put together some kind of attack plan?"

I frown at my sister, worried that she means that literally. Hopefully she doesn't plan to attack Granada Ruez.

"Sure. I'll tell Granada you're here. By the way, I'm Lucinda." She then points to me. "And you're wearing a Granada Green jacket. One of the earlier designs."

"I got it a couple of years ago and I still love it. It's so comfortable."

"Cool." Lucinda smiles as she heads for a door in back.

"Right . . . *cool*." Paige rolls her eyes at me. "You know how much I hate that jacket, Erin."

"Be quiet," I warn.

"It's frumpy and not the least bit flattering."

"Are you going to keep this up?" I glance to the back of the showroom to be sure no one is listening.

She shrugs. "Hey, don't forget this is my show and it's supposed to be about fashion and style." She pulls a recycled denim dress from a rack, holding it out at arm's length as if she's afraid it might bite her. "And this does not even come close to being fashionable or stylish. Good grief, no one — not even Kate Moss — could make this rag look good."

"Paige!" I hiss at her.

"Sorry, but you know how this gets to me, Erin."

"Just try to be polite, *please*."

"Fine, I'll be politely honest." She puts the dress back and sighs. "But I can't promise you that Granada Greenwear will get a spot on the show. Unless I use it in my *fashion don'ts* segment."

"Why can't you think positively?" I ask. "What about protecting the environment or fair treatment of overseas workers? Both are issues that Granada respects and fights for. Doesn't that mean anything to you?"

"Of course." Paige nods. "You know I'm totally for that. But it's too bad Granada's focusing her efforts in the *fashion* industry." Paige pulls out a baggy-looking pair of drawstring pants and frowns. "She might be better off making home décor products. Like this fabric would be nice for, say, a couch slipcover." She chuckles. "And these pants are almost big enough."

"Those pants look comfortable to me." I take them from her and feel the fabric. "See how soft this is." I read the label. "Bamboo fibers," I tell her. "A renewable resource with very little negative impact on the planet."

"The negative impact comes when someone walks down the street wearing those hippo pants." She laughs. "Hey, I think I'll use that line on the show."

"Maybe we should just forget the whole thing." I put the pants back on the rack. "If you're going to make fun of Granada Ruez, I refuse to be involved."

"So you want to leave then? Just make some excuse and get out of here?"

I just shrug, feeling totally deflated.

Now Paige almost looks contrite. "Hey, I'm sorry, Erin," she says quietly. "I got carried away. I didn't mean to rain on your parade."

"Yeah ... well ... not everyone is into your brand of *haute couture* style. Some of us are quite happy to be comfortable and environmentally aware. Why can't *On the Runway* cater to those types too? I just read that there's going to be an earth-friendly design show during Fashion Week in New York. They seem to get the importance of it, and I, for one, plan to be there for it."

"I've got it!" Paige exclaims.

"What?"

"You can do the Granada Greenwear interview yourself. And you can be our *On the Runway* conservation expert. That way I won't sound like a complete hypocrite by giving my thumbs-up to bad style."

"But I'm supposed to be *behind* the camera, remember?"

"It's your choice, Erin. If you want to pursue this idea of green fashion, you'll have to do it in *front* of the camera." She holds up a patchwork shirt and just shakes her head. "Because I simply cannot force myself to pretend that I like this granola wear."

We hear laughter from behind us and I turn to see Granada and Lucinda standing nearby. "Did you just hear all that?" I ask lamely.

Granada nods. "And don't worry, it's not the first time I've experienced that reaction. I'm fully aware that Granada Greenwear is not for everyone. We don't even want to be." Granada is Demi Moore meets Whoopi Goldberg—or maybe I'm thinking of the old film *Ghost*. But she has delicate features, expressive eyes, and these wild-looking brown dreadlocks that reach halfway down her back. And, although she's a lot more bohemian than I could ever be, she's very stylish.

"I *love* your clothes," I say in all earnestness.

"But your sister does not." Granada frowns as she takes in Paige's outfit. "And unfortunately you appear to love designers who *don't* love our planet. Why is that?" She comes closer and looks into Paige's eyes. "Do you like the idea of small children working ten hours or more a day, seven days a week, in disgusting conditions, just so you can wear those fancy clothes? Or perhaps you don't mind that toxic fabric dyes and chemicals—the ones used to make your pretty little outfit—contribute to the harmful runoff that pollutes waterways and wildlife? Some of the very water sources that the poor need just to survive? Is that the price you think should be paid just so someone like you can look *chic*?"

Paige, for once in her life, is speechless.

"I told her not to wear that outfit," I say to Granada.

Granada just smiles. "I'm sure she only wore it to get my hackles up. And it's worked."

"I wish I had my camera on while you were talking," I tell Granada. "Paige is usually the one dishing out the criticism!"

She waves her hand. "I say things like that all the time—especially when I'm talking to the skeptics."

"I don't mind protecting the planet," Paige finally says. "I just won't call something unattractive stylish."

"But don't you think style, like beauty, is in the eyes of the beholder?" Granada gives Paige a quick head-to-toe glance.

"Yes, I suppose you're right." Paige stands a bit straighter. "But *On the Runway* is my show, so I guess that makes me the beholder. And, I'm sorry, but I wouldn't be caught dead in these clothes."

Fortunately Granada just laughs again.

"But what if someone died making your clothes?" I challenge my sister.

Her brow creases. "Well, that would make me sad. But I don't think that's really the—"

"Don't be so sure," Granada tells her. "In fact, why don't you check out my website to see for yourself? I have a number of articles there about pollution and inhumane practices in foreign countries. You might be surprised at what goes on … all in the name of fashion."

I turn to Paige. "I think I'll take you up on your offer. I would like to interview Granada myself."

"I can't promise you that it'll air," Paige tells me. She nods to the front door where Fran, our director, and the rest of our crew are just coming in. "But you can give it your best shot and see what Helen says when she sees it."

And that is exactly what I do. For the next hour I interview Granada about her design work as well as her concern for the planet. Paige even helps me to rephrase some questions so they come out better. And then we actually film a conversation between Granada and Paige, very similar to the one they had earlier. My sister cooperates, playing the shallow fashionista (complete with her witty pokes at bad style and her ignorance about green issues) as Granada educates her about some atrocities going on in other countries.

When I'm done with the interview two things surprise me: First, I pulled this interview off, being comfortable in front of the camera instead of hiding behind it. Second, Fran seems to think that me as *Runway's* conservation expert could be a good segment.

"I have an invitation for you," Granada tells me as we're packing up to go.

"What's that?"

"Come be in my fashion show next week."

"Me?" *Okay, this woman must be really desperate for models.* "Uh, did you notice my height?"

She laughs. "My models are from all walks of life, Erin. You are a beautiful girl and you would fit in perfectly. Trust me."

Paige lets out a giggle and it's not hard to guess what she's thinking.

"Fine," I say in aggravation. "I'll be in your fashion show. And I'll ask our producer if we can film some of it for our show."

"That'd be great." Granada hands me a brochure. "As you can see we have some well-known models participating too. Everyone's time is being donated because the proceeds are going to FIFTI."

"Fifty what?" Paige asks in interest.

"F-I-F-T-I," Granada explains. "Fashion in Fair Trade Industries. We used to have fifty members, but thankfully we've gotten even bigger."

"Oh?" Paige points to a name on the brochure I'm holding. "Is Sunera really going to be in your show?"

"Of course." Granada nods.

"Who's that?" I ask.

"One of the top models in the industry," Paige informs me. "She was born in Nigeria. Totally gorgeous. Internationally famous. Just about the hottest thing in fashion."

"She's flying in from Paris just for this event," Granada says.

Paige is still studying the brochure. "You have quite a lineup here."

"All women who care about fair trade and preserving the planet."

"Some of them are a bit past their prime," Paige says, "but impressive all the same." She hands me back the brochure now. "You *are* in good company, Erin."

Suddenly all my insecurities kick in. "I don't know," I say to Granada. "Maybe it's not such a good idea for me to model for your show. I mean, I've never done anything like that before and I'm totally inex —"

"Nonsense," she tells me. "You'll be great."

I glance at Paige, wishing she'd save me from myself. "You'll be fine, Erin," she says in a congenial way. "In fact, it'll be good for you."

"Hey, why don't you do it too?" I suggest hopefully. "It could be Paige Forrester from *On the Runway* actually *on* the runway."

Paige laughs. "I seriously doubt that Granada would want me for her—"

"Don't be so sure." Granada holds a finger in the air. "In fact, I am getting an idea ... or perhaps it's more of a challenge."

"What?" Paige almost looks interested.

"You seem convinced that green fashion equals bad fashion, right?"

Paige shrugs with a coy expression, like, duh, the answer is obvious.

"So how about if I put together an outfit that I think you'd actually *want* to wear—I mean out in public. And if you like it well enough, you must agree to model it in my fashion show."

"Do you think that's even possible?" Paige frowns. "I've looked around your shop and I'm sure your clothes appeal to *some* people. But I'm not exactly an earth muffin, you know."

"I know." Granada seems to be thinking. "But I'd like to prove that green fashion can be high fashion."

"Just keep in mind that I've got a reputation to maintain," Paige says. "I'm known for being bluntly honest when it comes to style. And I refuse to act like I love some eco-fashion outfit when I really don't."

"Are you willing to give it a try?"

Paige seems to be considering it. "Sure. Why not?"

So they shake hands and it's like the green gauntlet's been

thrown. And while I like that Paige is giving this a fair shot, I'm worried for Granada's sake. I know my sister's influence is growing. What if Paige humiliates Granada on our show? And, if she does, will it be my fault? Will I be to blame if green fashion goes backward in the minds of some of our viewers?

# Chapter 2

"*I agree with you, Erin,*" *Blake tells* me as he drives us to our college fellowship group at church, "but I can see Paige's side too. She's all about style and if she compromises herself, well, it might weaken the show."

"But there are all kinds of styles," I argue.

"Absolutely. But your show—*On the Runway*—sets the fashion bar high, which your viewers now expect. And you have to hand it to Paige—she knows how to deliver."

"Man, you sound just like Helen Hudson now."

"Hey, thanks, I'll take that as a compliment."

I don't admit that it was meant as a slam. "Maybe *you* should be a producer too," I say teasingly.

I enjoy talking with Blake like this, but I'm still not sure that I'm doing the right thing by giving Blake another chance. I keep telling myself that if he breaks my heart again, I will walk away and never look back. I just hope I'm not fooling myself.

I know that my friend Lionel Stevens doesn't think too highly of Blake. In fact, sometimes he's downright rude—

even in fellowship group. Like last week, all three of us were talking and Lionel just walked away. It surprised me, because that's not exactly how Jesus tells us to treat each other. What about forgiveness and second chances? Maybe Lionel is just being protective of me. Why are these things never simple?

"I wish I could be a producer." Blake shakes his head. "I told my dad I was thinking about switching schools and changing my major to film and TV, and his face got so red, I thought he was going to have a stroke or something. He wouldn't even speak to me. Then he had my mom inform me they don't plan to support me for the rest of my life."

"Ouch."

"Tell me about it."

"I guess I should be thankful for my mom."

"Sure, but you're an industry kid, Erin. You kind of grew up in TV land."

I laugh. "That sounds like I'm stuck in some old rerun. Like maybe *The Beverly Hillbillies*. I used to be addicted to that show in grade school. Paige used to worry that Elly May was my role model."

"I don't mean TV Land the network, silly. I mean having parents who work in TV. With a news anchor dad and producer mom, you practically grew up on Channel Five news, so of course your mom would encourage you." He pauses. "Your dad too ... if he was alive."

"Yeah ... I sometimes wonder what he'd think of our show."

"He'd be proud of you, Erin."

As Blake pulls into the church parking lot I'm not so sure. Maybe Dad would be proud of Paige since she's actually chasing her dreams. Dad used to tell us to dream big ... and then to go after those dreams. As for me, well, I'm not even sure what my dream is anymore. Recently it feels like I'm just tagging along with Paige while she pursues her dream career.

We get out of the car and I spot Tony and Mollie. We wave and call out, hurrying across the lot to catch up with them. I'm still feeling cautious about my "best" friend Mollie these days. It's like something in her has changed these past few weeks. It's kind of like she's pushing me away, or keeping me at arm's length. I know she's been jealous over the show—she even admitted as much. Yet it's hard to believe that would make her edge me out the way she has lately. And maybe she should get over it. I mean, I know she wants to break into acting, and that can be frustrating because it's a cutthroat, competitive world. But if you suffer from jealousy or can't take rejection, you should just get out.

"What's up, *Runway*?" she says as we walk toward the church together. Tony and Blake are discussing the possibility of going to a Lakers game next week. I've been pretending I don't mind the nickname she's been calling me lately, but it's starting to get old.

"Not much, *Commercial Queen*," I jab back—as in *hint-hint*.

But she just frowns. "That's not funny."

"Sorry." I force a smile. "So, how's it really going, Mollie? How's school? How's life?"

"Same as usual."

"Any auditions?"

"Not really."

Then, to change the subject and because I know she used to be into green fashion, I decide to tell her about Granada Ruez. I give her the quick rundown on Paige's fashion snobbery and how I actually did the interview. "And get this," I finally say. "Granada even invited me to be in her fashion show."

Mollie laughs. "No way. Is she doing a show for short people? Maybe she'd like me to model too."

Then I tell her about the lineup of professionals. "Talk about intimidating," I admit. "I really wanted to back out when I heard who was in it."

"Oh, that *would* be hard. I wonder why she wants *you* to model anyway. You think it's just to get on your TV show?"

"Maybe, but she knows I'm a fan." Okay, I hear Mollie's jab plain and clear, but I know it's probably just jealousy. "I suppose Granada *might've* been trying to win favors ... or maybe she was just being nice." Then I tell Mollie about Paige accepting Granada's challenge. "So there's a slim possibility that Paige will be in the fashion show too."

"I'll believe it when I see it," she says as we enter the building.

"Yeah, me too." As we head into the fellowship hall I'm thinking maybe Mollie is back to her old self, or maybe I just imagined the whole chill-factor thing. But then our other friends come and gather around us. Suddenly they're talking about the *Malibu Beach* show that Paige and I were on and the Golden Globes runway that we walked and, as I respond, Mollie sort of slinks off to the sidelines like she's unwanted, which is perfectly ridiculous. And I think—what am I supposed to do right now? Just ignore everyone but Mollie? Tell them it's none of their business and to take a hike? And why is Mollie acting so weird anyway? As if to make things worse, she sits down in the front, where we usually like to sit together, but only saves one seat for Tony, and by the time Blake and I sit down (after fielding questions from Paige's fan club), the only seats left are clear in the back.

I know Christians aren't perfect, but it seems like we

should be kinder to each other, and that we shouldn't be too easily offended. Of course, even as I say this, I realize that I'm offended too. But I actually think I have a right to feel offended since Mollie, my supposed best friend, keeps treating me like this. The truth is I'm so offended that I can barely focus on the worship time now. But then, when we're praying, I silently ask God to help me with Mollie ... and for us to forgive each other if necessary. And it does seem necessary.

But as soon as the message ends and the meeting breaks up, Mollie and Tony just take off instead of sticking around for refreshments and fellowship. They don't even say good-bye.

"What's with them?" I ask Blake.

"Huh?" He pauses with a tortilla chip halfway to his mouth.

"Tony and Mollie. It's like they just keep to themselves lately. I don't get it."

Blake just shrugs then bites into the chip. "Maybe they just needed to get home early."

I nod like that might be it, but I'm thinking it's probably not. My guess is that Mollie is punishing me. By shutting me out, I wonder if she thinks she's teaching me a lesson.

So when I get home, I decide to just get this out into the open via email. I write my note quickly. I tell her that she's hurt my feelings a lot lately, that it seems like we're barely friends, and that I'd like to know what's up. And then I hit send even more quickly. Of course, now I wonder ... will the email come across all wrong and end up hurting Mollie? Was it too aggressive? Hopefully not, because it wasn't my intent to hurt her. Still, hasn't Mollie been hurting me? And intention-ally too, it seems. The best thing is to just get it out there and then deal with it. At least that's how we used to handle our differences . . .

A couple days passed without a response from Mollie. At first I checked my email obsessively. Then I considered calling her, but I'd already tried to communicate with her. She obviously didn't care whether or not we were still best friends. Maybe we're not friends at all anymore. But it seems I have gotten so busy with the show that I don't have much time to worry about it.

"I can't believe there are this many top designers in LA," I tell Paige as we go to yet another designer's studio on Tuesday. It's the last one of the day, and I hope we're not too late.

"They're all from the list that Helen sent Fran." Paige grimaces as she turns onto a derelict street in what we already determined was a slightly questionable neighborhood.

"Who is this designer anyway?" I question. "Maybe I put the address in wrong." I look at the GPS and then back at the paper in my hand. "Or maybe Fran's assistant got it wrong. Although Leah usually gets everything right."

"Apparently she got this right too." Paige points ahead. "There's the van. This is the place."

"So who's this George Mabin guy anyway? I've never heard of him."

"Besides your buddy Granada, you've never heard of most designers, Erin. You barely know Valentino, Gucci, or Prada."

"Maybe it's because they don't impress me that much."

But once we're inside, I quickly realize that I *am* impressed with George Mabin. His studio is one of the coolest I've seen. This guy is into color and graphics big-time. I pull out my camera and start trying to catch everything I can while he and Paige talk about his designs. Every garment is like a work of art. Some look native with mixtures of animal prints and tribal designs. Others are more like modern art with colored blocks and angles. "My grandmother raised me," he tells Paige during the interview segment. "She was really into African culture so her whole apartment was like this natural-art museum."

"That must explain some of the items here in your studio," Paige observes, motioning her hand to a white wall where a number of African artifacts—including large colorful shields, batik fabrics, and dramatic carvings—are displayed.

"My grandmother left everything she owned to me when she passed a few years ago. I like keeping it around me now."

"I'm sorry for your loss." Paige nods toward a rack of his latest designs—the ones he just gave us a sneak preview of. "But I'm guessing your grandmother's influence is still going strong. Does it show up in your work?"

"Absolutely. She's my inspiration. She's the one who sent me to design school and helped me get started when it looked like a hopeless uphill battle."

"Tell us about why you located your studio here ... in this part of town."

"Well, besides cheap real estate, you mean?" He grins. "You see, this neighborhood here, it's also a part of my roots. Something I need to remember, because I got kind of rebellious as a teen. I thought I was so smart ... and that my grandmother was overly protective. I started hanging with some really bad kids—gangbanger types, you know. Anyway, I got myself into some big trouble, which included juvenile detention for about a year ... but it also gave me time to figure some things out." He chuckles. "The best thing about the gang was doing graffiti.

It was my first experience with art and design, and I continued playing with it while I was in juvie. Then I got out and realized how much I loved art. And when my grandmother recognized I had talent, she encouraged me to really go for it."

"Some people in the design world don't take you seriously if you don't live in New York," Paige continues. It's a lead-up to a question she's asked all the LA designers. "What do you have to say to that?"

He nods. "I tried New York for a while, but it didn't work for me. I had to come back here to get the creative juices flowing. And even if I miss out on some opportunities back East, I have to live my own life, you know. If I'm not happy, my designs aren't happy either."

With my camera, I zoom in on his face. His dark eyes are sparkling and it's obvious that he's totally passionate about his work, and that he enjoys his life. And I think—that's what I want too. I want the career that makes me most happy. Will it always be filming for *On the Runway*? I doubt it. And yet I know there's still a lot to be learned. I also think it's going to be a process—a series of experiences—before I find out who I really am or what I'm really good at. But I do want to get there. I want to chase my dreams.

"George is a cool guy," I say to Paige as she drives us home.

"And a good designer too. Not really my style, but I can see why he's so popular."

"So you can admit that good design reaches beyond your own personal taste and style?"

"Of course. I never said it didn't."

"But what about Granada Greenwear?"

"Like I told you, Erin, I don't see *that* as good design. The kinds of clothes Granada makes wouldn't look good on anybody. But George Mabin is different. His clothes look fantastic on the right women. Not me, I know. But you saw the photos in his studio. Those clothes, those women, those vibrant colors and dramatic styles ... they were absolutely drop-dead gorgeous. I'm glad Helen put him on the list."

I guess I'm not really surprised that Paige liked his designs. I should've known she can see past cultural differences and appreciate a really talented designer. But that only makes me more concerned about Granada Greenwear. Maybe Paige is right. Maybe that really isn't good design. But I can't think of anything worse than giving an eco-friendly designer a black eye on our show when, more than ever, I believe that we need to think more globally ... and respect the planet.

# Chapter

## 3

*When we preview this week's show* — the one featuring local designers in their studios — I'm pleasantly surprised to see that Granada Greenwear has made the final cut. And although I don't think I'm terribly brilliant at interviewing — I'm not the natural that my sister is, anyway — I think I did okay.

"Another great show," Helen says as the lights come back on. "Good work, girls. And I think Paige stumbled onto something, Erin."

"What's that?"

"Letting you do the less-stylish fashion spots."

"Gee, thanks."

Helen just laughs as she leads the way out of the viewing room and toward the conference area where she's asked us to reconvene. She's not exactly a hands-on kind of producer. Mostly she's the one who finds the money and works out the contracts with the networks — and she knows everyone who is anyone. But I know she likes to feel involved since this show was her baby to start with. "You girls know that any way we can increase our viewership is okay with me. And our sponsors too." She turns to one of the lesser producers, a young woman who's worked her way up from an assistant position and seems a little unsure of her new role. "You should be looking for some sponsors who'll appreciate our new global focus, Leslie."

Leslie makes note of this as we settle around the big conference table, and the group of producers and assistants as well as Fran begin to chat amongst themselves about which companies to consider. Finally Helen turns back to us. "So, girls, how's next week's New York show coming together?"

"It's looking great," Paige tells her. "We've been working on a killer lineup, although I haven't seen the final list yet."

Helen turns to the director. "How many fashion shows do you plan to cover?"

"Well, as you know, the timing is perfect," Fran explains. "With everyone getting geared for Fashion Week, there are some dress rehearsals going on around town. Right now I have about six shows to choose from. Unfortunately some of the dates overlap, so we'll need to pick and choose." Then she rattles off the list of designers and I realize that Granada Greenwear isn't on it.

"Don't forget Granada Ruez," I remind her. "I'm actually going to be in that show. And maybe Paige too."

Helen frowns. "Oh, I think that's one we can safely leave off the list, Erin."

"But I promised Granada," I protest.

"Yes, but we only have so much time," Fran points out.

"But what about green sponsors?" I question Helen. "Or about increasing our viewership?"

"And did you know that Sunera is going to be in Granada's show?" Paige tosses me a bone here. "That alone makes it newsworthy, don't you think?"

"Sunera Makewa?" Helen looks shocked. "She's doing Granada's show?"

"For free," I add. I explain how the proceeds will benefit FIFTI. "So it's actually a good cause too."

"Okay." Helen nods and both she and Fran make changes to their lists. "Granada Greenwear too. Good grief, you girls are going to be busy for the next week."

"And then the following Thursday it's off to New York — for the *real* Fashion Week," Fran announces happily. "Leah's already got it all booked."

"That's right," Leah confirms. Leah just graduated from film school, something I barely started, and yet Leah's job is pretty much to keep Paige and me comfortable and happy and successful. Fran's made it clear numerous times that if we need anything, we call Leah and she will deliver. If I think about it too hard, it almost hurts my head. "I'll email you the itinerary in a day or two," Leah promises. "I'm still working on the hotel, which is a challenge to say the least. I'm hoping you won't have to switch hotels midstream, but Fashion Week really ties that town into knots."

"But Fashion Week doesn't start until the following week," Helen points out. "What's the big rush?"

"I want the girls there early to interview the New York designers," Fran explains.

Helen looks skeptical. "Do you seriously think the New York designers will give you the time of day during the week before their big event?"

"I've already talked to a couple of designers who are interested." Fran looks down at her notebook. "I think we've got the Olsen twins on board too, right, Leah?"

Leah nods. "And I've got some good tips on some of the

newest and possibly hottest models, and I'm thinking they should be eager for some airtime. We're lining up some of the morning news shows and—"

"Oh, I just remembered something." Helen holds a finger in the air importantly. "My good friend Eva Perez has a daughter, Taylor Mitchell, who's modeling in New York. And I want you girls to meet her and have her on the show."

"You mean Eva Perez the singer?" Fran asks.

"That's right."

"So is Eva's daughter any good as a model, or is this just a friendly goodwill gesture on your part?" Fran looks dubious.

"From what I hear, Taylor is considered to be quite good."

"I know who that is," Paige says suddenly. "Taylor Mitchell originally modeled exclusively for Dylan Marceau, not long after his debut. She was eighteen and just out of high school. But she quickly became such a hot commodity that she can work for anyone now. And, trust me, the girl is absolutely gorgeous—she does both print and runway."

Helen smiles at Paige. "It's lovely to know that someone is doing her homework."

Paige beams at the compliment.

"So, here's what I'm thinking, girls. What if you actually stayed in the apartment with Taylor and her roommate for a night or two? I mean stay there *with* cameras running, like a reality show—a day or two in the life of a supermodel. I ran this idea by Eva the other night at dinner, and she said that thanks to Taylor's roommate's healthy budget, the apartment is quite large and luxurious. At least according to Manhattan standards. So you should be comfortable."

"Well, aside from the cameras running," I say. "I assume they won't be running twenty-four seven."

"No, I'm sure they'll let you use the bathroom in private." Helen winks at me.

"Do you really think Taylor and her roommate would agree to this?"

"Eva confided to me that the roommate, the one whose parents actually own the apartment, really wants to make it in fashion. And that she'd probably be glad to have you girls there ... if she can get some good airtime on your show. My guess is that Taylor will be okay since it was her mom who helped hatch this idea."

Paige nods. "This could be awesome."

"Now the plan is to do this *after* Fashion Week," Helen explains. "The girls won't be as busy by then, but it will still be a nice little slice of their life. Then we'll run it as our follow-up show after the actual Fashion Week episode. And after that, we'll zip you girls back here to do the red carpet at the Oscars. How does that sound?"

The truth is I think it all sounds rather exhausting. I can't even wrap my mind around it. But Paige seems to take this, like the rest of this business, in stride, and I guess if she can keep up, I can too. After all, she's the one with the most pressure to perform.

"And I think we can milk two or more episodes out of Fashion Week alone," Fran is telling Helen now. "The first show will focus on the designers in their studios, the models as they prepare and all that. It will be a great buildup for the next show — the actual Fashion Week show."

"Great!" Helen claps her hands. "We'll get at least three shows out of New York then. Brilliant."

Paige and I are kept über-busy during the following week, literally running all over town to attend the local fashion shows. But the payoff is that these events are actually a lot easier than the previous week when we were interviewing designers. Mostly our crew just films snippets of the shows. (We're not allowed to film too much since it seems most designers suffer from a serious paranoia that someone is going to steal their designs.) Then Paige does some quick interviews behind the scenes. Meanwhile, I mostly hang out with my camera, try to look necessary, and practice filming.

But on Saturday morning, we have to make an appearance at Granada's studio for our fitting session. This is to be followed by a dress rehearsal for the show, which is scheduled for Sunday afternoon — just one part of LA's pre-Fashion-Week warm-up. As I park my Jeep with Paige fidgeting next to me, I realize the pressure is on. And everything could easily go wrong.

"I am not looking forward to this," Paige warns me as we stand outside the studio, waiting for Lucinda to come and unlock the door so we can go inside.

"Just be a good sport," I say.

"The hardest part is that I really don't want to offend her."

"Seriously?" I have to laugh at the ludicrousness of this. "Since when has that stopped you before?"

"Well, I like her. And I like the things she stands for too."

Go figure. But it does give me hope. For Paige, that is. I'm not so sure about this fashion show. Soon we are inside where a number of the other models are trying on clothes, not including Sunera, who isn't due to arrive until this evening.

"What? No cameras today?" Lucinda smiles as she hands

me several hangers' worth of clothing, wrapped in what I'm guessing is a recycled sheet.

"We'll save that for tomorrow," Paige tells her.

"Granada wants you to meet her in back," Lucinda says to Paige.

The room is buzzing with girls trying on outfits and cooperating with seamstresses and stylists. I learn that I'm only expected to model one ensemble, a huge relief because I doubt that I'd be coordinated enough to perform the quick changes I've seen models make during a fast-paced show. I'm sure Lucinda realizes that I'm slightly fashion-challenged, so she sticks around to help me and make sure I get the pieces on right.

"I love it," I tell Lucinda when I emerge from the dressing room for my final inspection. The A-line skirt is made from recycled men's ties that look like they're from the fifties. It has an asymmetrical hemline that actually seems to make me look taller. And this is topped with a white blouse created with pieces of patchwork lace, again recycled fabric, with a pure organic cotton camisole underneath and a fitted black wool vest on top.

"That vest is made from a recycled sweater that was boiled to shrink the knit tightly like that," Lucinda informs me. "And the buttons are from the forties."

"I really love it," I tell her as I look in the mirror. "I might have to buy the whole thing."

She grins. "I'm sure that can be arranged." Then she helps me with a red belt, which is made from a recycled seatbelt and old rodeo buckle. And my shoes are a pair of red Mary-Jane clogs made from hemp and vegetable dyed. I know Paige wouldn't be caught dead in these shoes, but I think they're fantastic. Not to mention comfortable.

"Well, I'm a happy camper," I assure Lucinda. "If it's okay, I'll look around to see how the other models are doing."

"And I'll check on your sister." Lucinda's anxious expression is probably reflective of mine. "Hopefully it's not going too badly."

I walk around the room and am surprised to see that there's really quite a variety of styles going on. Something for everyone. I even ask the models about how they like the garments and wish I had my camera as I hear, again and again, how comfortable, how breathable, how soft the materials are.

"I'm so used to suffering when I model," a pale redhead tells me. "I just expect to be tortured during the fitting right up until the runway. But Granada's clothes are delightful. I already have a few pieces in my closet and by tomorrow, I expect to have a few more."

And so it goes. I decide that even if Paige hates her outfit, at least she can get some good quotes from the other models tomorrow. Then I hear Granada calling my name, and the next thing I know I'm ushered into the back room where Paige is wearing white linen pants — that fit perfectly — topped with a recycled lace blouse similar to mine, only longer and worn as a jacket, with a pale blue camisole underneath. Her sandals and low-slung belt are both made of natural hemp. I think she looks great.

"I love that outfit," I tell her.

She nods at Granada. "I have to admit it's really comfortable."

"Something you could wear on an island vacation or just out to lunch with the girls," Granada suggests.

"Or on the runway tomorrow." Paige grins.

Granada's brows lift. "So I've managed to convince you then?"

Paige fingers the lace on her blouse. "I won't say I'm a total convert, but I guess green doesn't have to be frumpy."

"And you'll do my show?" Granada looks hopeful.

"For sure." Paige nods.

"And we're pretty sure your fashion show will be on *Runway* next week," I tell her.

"But we can't make promises," Paige reminds me. "That's up to the editors."

"But I pleaded your case," I say.

Granada doesn't seem concerned. "C'est la vie."

I let out a sigh as Granada goes to check on something with one of the models. Catastrophe averted. Paige may never laud Granada Greenwear as *haute couture*, but at least she's giving the line a fair shake.

We go through the paces of walking on the catwalk, and although Paige takes to it like a fish to water, it's harder than I expected. Finally Granada tells me to simply be myself. "Just relax, Erin," she urges me. "We'll let the audience know that you're not a pro."

"Maybe she should carry her camera," Paige teases. "That always puts her at ease."

Granada nods. "Great idea. Erin, you will carry your video camera. And I'll comment on that and how that's part of your persona for your show. It'll work just fine."

"And Erin could even pretend to be shooting footage of the audience," Paige suggests.

"Perfect." Granada grins at Paige. "Very fun."

"Only I won't be pretending," I tell them. "I'll really be filming and maybe it'll end up on next week's show." At least that's how I hope it will go. I suppose there's always the possibility I could fall flat on my face. But at least we're not wearing stilettos.

By the time Paige and I head home later in the day, we're both feeling fairly positive about tomorrow's fashion event. "It might even be fun," I admit. "I really like the camera idea. Thanks for suggesting it."

"So what are you doing tonight?" Paige asks as I pull into the condo parking lot and snag a space.

"Fellowship group," I tell her as I turn off the engine. "Want to come?"

"Not this time."

"But you keep telling me that you're going to come sometime," I remind her. "Why not tonight?"

"Because I have a date tonight."

"A date? With who?"

"Benjamin."

"*Really?*" For some reason—I honestly don't know why, because I shouldn't be surprised—this floors me. Benjamin Kross might be the hottest thing on reality TV and the star of *Malibu Beach*, but I thought Paige had been hurt enough by him. And I had hoped that since he'd kind of faded into the woodwork lately, Paige had told him to take a hike.

"Yes. And don't get all grumpy about it."

"I'm not."

"I promised him the night of the Golden Globes that if he left me alone for two weeks, I'd consider going out with him."

"Even after what he did to you?" I still try to block out that horrible day when Benjamin Kross and Mia Renwick pulled their little stunt on *Malibu Beach*, acting like Paige had lied and cheated and attempted to break apart the "happy couple," when in reality Paige had turned out to be their publicity victim.

"I thought Christians were supposed to forgive people." She eyes me curiously as we walk up the stairs to our condo unit. "Are you ever going to forgive Benjamin?"

I shrug. I hate to admit that she's right. "I guess I have to ... if you do."

"Well, I have forgiven him. And, if it makes you feel any better, he's apologized so many times that I actually begged him to quit."

"So do you think he really learned his lesson?" I ask as we go inside.

"I seriously doubt that he'll ever do something like that again."

"Something like what?" Mom asks from the kitchen. "Who are we talking about?"

Paige fills her in on Benjamin and her two-week promise. "So tonight is the big night."

"I thought he was getting together with that dark-haired girl, the one on the show. Natalie or—"

"Natasha," Paige offers. "No, Mom, he said that was just Natasha chasing after him and the editors playing it up so that they could use some jealous shots of Mia. You know how it goes."

I study my mom. "You actually watched *Malibu Beach*?"

Mom chuckles. "Someone at work had recorded it and it was playing in the break room. I couldn't help myself."

"I recorded it here," Paige says with a smile. "I watched it too ... the next day."

I laugh and roll my eyes. "So I'm the only one in the family who didn't?"

"It's probably still in the TiVo," Paige tells me, "if you want to see it."

"No thanks." I wave my hand and head for my room.

"But you will forgive him?" Paige calls after me.

"Yes," I call back. But I'm thinking it will take more than two weeks before I forget what Benjamin did to my sister. And I'll probably be paying close attention to make sure he doesn't do it again. In fact, I might even start watching *Malibu Beach*. Or not.

# Chapter
## 4

*As I drive myself to fellowship group, I'm* surprised at how much I miss Blake and I selfishly wish he hadn't gone out of town for a family wedding. When I arrive, after fielding more curious questions from "fans"—which I admit is still really awkward for me—I also find myself missing Mollie and wondering why she and Tony aren't here tonight.

Then, as I listen to the sermon (although Kris, the pastor, calls it a "talk") I realize that his words really hit home. Forgiving others is like eating or sleeping; you have to do it on a regular, daily basis or risk getting sick. It's not the first time Kris has talked about forgiving others, and it's not the first time I've had to admit there's someone in my life I need to forgive. Possibly more than one someone. The first who comes to mind is Benjamin. Although I told Paige I'd forgive him, I realize I need to do this not just with words, but inside as well. Also, I need to forgive Mollie. But maybe even more importantly, I need to ask her to forgive me. And not via email either.

"I forgot to give you this ticket," Paige tells me as I'm getting ready for bed.

"What ticket?"

"Granada gave us each an extra ticket for the show tomorrow. You can invite a guest."

"Oh." I nod. "You think Mom wants to come?"

"I already asked her and she definitely would, except that she's going out with Jon."

"Maybe they both could come."

Paige nods. "Yeah, I suggested that too. But then she told me he somehow snagged a pair of tickets to *Mamma Mia* and I told her to forget it. I'd skip the fashion show myself just to see that show."

"You would not."

Paige chuckles. "Yeah, you're probably right. Anyway, here's your ticket. I invited Benjamin to come and, if you don't mind, he'll give me a ride home afterward. Okay?"

I should have seen *that* coming. "Sure. Whatever."

After Paige leaves, I decide to invite Mollie. I know it's late, but I also know she answers her cell phone later than this. But after a couple of rings, I am sent to voicemail.

"Hey, Mollie. I missed you at fellowship tonight. And I really wanted to tell you I'm sorry if that crazy email I sent last week offended you. I mostly just wanted to talk to you and to make sure we're still friends. We are, aren't we? Anyway, I have a spare ticket to the Granada Greenwear fashion show tomorrow. Remember I told you about it? So call me if you want to come. I can leave it at the front door for you. Okay ... bye." Then I hang up and wonder if she'll even bother to call back. So far she hasn't been too good at that; but then, neither have I. So I call back and leave a second message, saying that if I don't hear from her by tomorrow morning, I might just see if Blake wants to come.

My phone rings the next morning, but instead of Mollie, it's Blake. "Want a ride to church?" he asks pleasantly.

"If I was going, I would. But I have to be at the Granada event by noon and I think church would be cutting it too close."

"So you're still doing it then? Paige didn't pull the plug?"

I fill him in on the details and when he says he'd like to come, I tell him I just happen to have a spare ticket. "I left a message for Mollie," I say, "but I told her if she didn't claim it this morning, it would go to someone else." I don't admit that he was the one I'd been thinking of.

"All right. When does her offer officially expire?"

I consider this. "Well, maybe I should give her until ten since that's when church begins. Seems fair to think she'd have called me by then."

"Sounds fair to me."

"If I don't hear from her, I'll call and leave you a message with directions. The show doesn't start until two."

"And if I see Mollie at church, I won't remind her to call you." He chuckles. "That's kind of selfish though — especially in church."

"If Mollie wants to come, she'll call me."

Apparently Mollie does not want to come. Because at eleven, when Paige and I are getting ready to leave, I call Blake and tell him where the show is being held and that his ticket will be at the door.

"Hey, maybe Ben and Blake will want to hang together," Paige suggests as we're going down the stairs. The next thing I know she's on the phone and telling Benjamin to call Blake, and getting the number from me, and even making plans for the four of us to get something to eat afterward. "I know I'll be starved by then." She hangs up and smiles. "It's all settled."

But just before noon, just as I'm parking at the hotel where the show's being held, Mollie calls. "I got your message," she tells me with a sleepy voice.

"You're at home?" I ask.

"Yeah. I slept in—didn't make it to church. Tony and I went to a late movie and I didn't get home until almost one."

"Yeah ... and since I didn't hear back from you I sort of, well, I offered the ticket to Blake."

"That figures." Her tone is flat and tinged with anger.

"He called and he was all excited about it and Paige set it up for him to go with Benjamin and—"

"Paige is back with Benjamin?"

"Well, they just barely started—"

"I just feel so out of it when it comes to you, Erin. It's like I'm the last one on your list."

"You were the first one on my list," I tell her. "I called you—"

"Yeah, whatever. I gotta go. Thanks for the invitation anyway." Then she hangs up on me. Just like that.

I hold my phone out and shake it. "She is impossible!"

"Mollie?"

"Yes. She's all bent out of shape because—"

"I know, Erin. I heard the whole thing. Let it go. Mollie's just being a brat. Don't let her drag you into it."

"Yeah ... right." We're going inside now and I think that's easier said than done. She's already dragged me into it.

"And don't forget to turn off your phone during the show."

"Okay." I sigh as I turn my phone off. Paige is right. Mollie is being a brat. And maybe next time I'll just wait for her to come and apologize to me.

The fashion show is a great distraction from the Mollie drama. And between getting dressed, shooting some film footage, doing a few quick interviews, and finally trying to "just breathe" as I wait for my turn to literally go *on the runway*, I manage to put the drama behind me.

"Now remember," Paige tells me. "Just be camera girl, getting your shots and having a good time."

I nod. The plan is for me to follow Paige, and we'll share the catwalk briefly as I shoot a bit of her walk and Granada tells the audience about our little sister act on our TV show. Really, it should be fun. Or that's what I keep telling myself as I try to imagine *not* falling on my face.

And, thankfully, it pretty much goes as planned. The audience seems to enjoy our little skit and before I know it, I'm done. And it's not long before the whole fashion show, which seems to be a hit, is complete. I manage to get some good shots of Sunera and then Paige, and I score an interview with Sunera afterward. All in all, I think it was time well spent, and Fran and the rest of the crew agree. This is a huge relief, especially considering they had to give up part of their Sunday to do it.

Because we've been busy getting shots and interviews, Paige and I haven't had a chance to change our clothes like the other models. We're finally just heading back to do this when Granada stops us. "Thanks for everything, girls. You were a wonderful addition to our show."

"And you'll be a great addition to ours," Paige tells her. "I'm almost certain you won't be cut."

"Fantastic." Granada grins at me. "Now I want to make

another deal with you girls. At least with Erin. I'm not sure Paige will want in."

"What?" I ask eagerly.

"You keep the outfit."

"Seriously? I mean, I was actually going to buy it—if I could afford it, but—"

"You keep it on the condition that you wear it once on your show. Besides this one, okay?"

"No problem."

"And a little mention of my company in the final credits."

"Of course," I assure her. "We already do that for any designers who send clothes that are used."

She turns to Paige. "Same offer to you, but I promise not to be offended if you turn it down."

"Hey, I'm in," Paige tells her. "I can't wait until we do a spot in some tropical location, and I'll be wearing this for sure."

Granada shakes both our hands. "On behalf of Third World workers and plants and animals who have no voice, I thank you."

"We should be thanking you," I tell her.

"And I have someone who wants to meet you," Paige tells Granada. "Benjamin Kross from—"

"I know who Benjamin Kross is." Granada grins.

"And he thinks that *Malibu Beach* should do something green on their show," Paige says as she leads Granada out to where our guys are waiting. "And maybe their show will feature some of your designs."

I chuckle as I shut down my camera and slip it into my backpack. I'm sure Paige would love to make a recommendation for Mia's wardrobe too. Maybe that saggy denim dress that Paige made fun of last week.

To save time, and because we're both ravenous, Paige and I decide not to change back into our other clothes to go out with Benjamin and Blake. It turns out that Benjamin made reservations at a great new restaurant in Beverly Hills. And, even though I usually act like I don't enjoy it, I have to say that it can be kind of fun being pointed at and observed as if we're all celebrities. People are flashing their cell phones at us and both Paige and Benjamin are rushed for a couple of autographs. I'm actually relieved that I'm not the center of this limelight, but it's fun to witness. Plus the treatment from the restaurant staff is way better than usual.

"I could get used to this," Blake says after an oblivious girl asks him for his autograph as we're leaving.

"That's what you think now," Benjamin tells him as we wait for the parking valet to bring his car back around. "But if you had to live with it for a while you might think differently."

"I'm still enjoying it." Paige smiles and waves at a couple of teen girls who are gawking at us from a car that's slowly cruising down the street—obviously on the lookout for celebs.

"The time will come when you might like your privacy more," he warns her.

"It's the price you pay for fame," she says like she's got it all figured out. "You simply have to deal with it."

"I don't know … It's okay for now, but I'm not sure I'd want to live like this for too long," I admit.

Just then a dark van pulls up so quickly that one of the parking valets jumps to avoid being hit. And—bam—just like that, several guys leap out with cameras and begin snapping as if they think they just caught something really earthshaking.

"And then you have the paparazzi." Benjamin just shakes his head.

"Let's give them what they want," Paige says quickly, turning to give them a great big smile. Benjamin follows suit, as do Blake and I. And the photographers sort of back off, like maybe that wasn't really what they were going for after all. Then they wave and hop back in their van and take off—probably in pursuit of more interesting celebs.

"See," Paige says in a matter-of-fact tone. "That wasn't so hard."

Benjamin laughs as he tips the valet. "No, it wasn't."

As Benjamin drives us back to the hotel to pick up Paige's car, I'm thinking once again that my sister really is cut out for this kind of high-profile lifestyle. She actually seems to fit in—and she genuinely loves it. Whether or not she'll always feel that way is anybody's guess, but for the moment she appears perfectly content.

And just because being photographed by crazed photographers is not my favorite pastime doesn't mean I should judge Paige for liking it. Still, I hope that I figure out what it is that makes me as happy as she seems to be today. I want the chance to chase my dreams too.

# Chapter 5

*"So how was the big fashion event?"* Mom asks as soon as she's in the door Sunday evening. Paige and I are in the middle of watching some of the film that I shot today.

"See for yourself," I tell Mom.

"Unedited, uncut, and uncensored," Paige quips.

"Does it need censoring?" Mom puts her purse down and comes over.

"Well, maybe some of the behind the scenes stuff," I admit. "I mean, girls were getting dressed, and they might not enjoy being seen in their underwear."

"Some of them would," Paige teases.

"Anyway, you can get a better idea of how it was when you see Friday's show," I tell her.

"Oh, Paige." Mom points to the TV where Paige is striding down on the catwalk. "You look like such a natural on that runway. I'm surprised that other designers didn't ask you to model for them as well."

"Erin did great too," Paige tells her.

"Aw thanks," I say. "But sorry, Mom—you can't see me here, because *I'm* behind the camera."

"You'll see her in the real show." Paige says. "She was fabulous."

I roll my eyes and turn off the TV after the footage comes to an end. "So how was *Mamma Mia*?" I ask Mom.

"Fantastic." Mom is heading to the kitchen. "I think I'll start some dinner. Anyone want to help?"

"And how is Jon?" Paige asks as we join Mom in the kitchen.

"Jon is fantastic too." Mom almost seems starry eyed as she sets a head of lettuce on the counter.

"Are you in love?" Paige pauses from reaching into the fridge to study Mom and I'm wishing she hadn't asked that. I'm not even sure I want to know the answer.

"Oh ... I don't know." Mom smiles mysteriously. "It's a little early for that."

"But you *do* like him, don't you?" Paige persists. "A lot, right?"

Mom looks embarrassed now. "He's a very nice man."

"I'll make the salad," I offer, taking the lettuce from Mom, trying to divert attention away from my blushing mother. I start jabbering on about how we went with Benjamin and Blake to this new restaurant and how the paparazzi snagged some photos and how Paige just waved and smiled.

"It's probably more fun for them when they have to chase you down to get a shot," Mom says as she pours rice into the boiling water. "So you've been out with Benjamin a couple of times now, Paige. How's that going?"

"It's okay," Paige tells her. "But I'm taking it nice and slow."

"And you and Blake?" Mom asks me. "Are you two a couple again?"

"I'm taking it even slower than Paige," I say with a chuckle. "Blake, for now, is my good friend. I told him that he's getting closer to boyfriend status all the time."

Mom laughs. "Good for you. Make him prove himself. Make them both prove themselves."

"I remember how Dad always told us not to settle for less than the best for guys as well as in life." I pause from slicing a tomato. "And I seriously want to stick to that."

"Me too!" Paige agrees.

"So do I," Mom says.


Later, as we sit down to eat, Mom asks about our plans for our New York trip. "Is everything falling into place?"

"Seems to be," Paige tells her. "We fly out Thursday—"

"This Thursday?" Mom looks surprised.

"Yep. Remember Fran wanted us out there a week early to interview designers and put together footage that will play before our Fashion Week show?"

"Yes I remember. But Thursday just seems so soon." Mom sighs. "I wish I could go with you girls."

"Why don't you?" Paige suggests.

"Oh, you know I can't get off work. Besides, you girls need to do this on your own. It's your show. You don't need your old mom meddling with it." But even as she says this, I sense that she regrets not being involved. I remember when Helen Hudson offered Mom a chance to help produce our show.

"You're not our *old* mom." I take her hand.

"And we would love it if you came along," Paige adds.

"Well, as long as you didn't try to direct the show or anything. Fran might not like that too much."

Mom laughs. "Thanks, honey. But you'll be fine without me tagging along. Just make sure I get a full itinerary before you take off."

"I'll remind Leah to copy you on all that," Paige promises.

After dinner, I head to my room to unwind. Eventually I decide to give Mollie a call. I have no idea if she'll even speak to me, but I really want to be mature about this and at least attempt to make things right. But, once again, I am sent directly to voicemail, and this time I don't bother to leave a message. For one thing, I'm getting aggravated that she seems to be ignoring my calls, but the other reason is that I'm worried I'll say something dumb and make things worse. Sometimes it's just better to keep your mouth shut.

Paige and I end up spending the next three days at the studio with Fran and the crew. Fran spends this time mapping out our time in New York as well as briefing us and planning our wardrobe.

"Hopefully we'll pick up more pieces once we get there," she informs us as the wardrobe workers pack the boxes to be sent on ahead to our hotel. "Leah let the designers know your sizes as well as sent DVDs of your show. But a lot of this we'll simply have to play by ear." She chuckles as she hands us a hard copy of our schedules. "And, after all, isn't that the beauty of reality TV?"

"Have you figured out how many of our crew will be coming yet?" Paige asks as she looks at the schedule.

"Thanks to a serious lack of available hotel rooms next week, that's a tough one—but Leah's on it. She might even stick the crew in New Jersey during Fashion Week proper.

 MARION CARNEGIE LIBRARY
206 SOUTH MARKET
MARION, IL 62959

And if we have to go bare-boned for a few days, in regard to our regular hair and makeup artists, I'll be counting on you, Paige. You seem to be a natural anyway."

"You mean I'll be doing my own hair and makeup?" Paige looks shocked and slightly diva-like as she says this.

"I hope that won't happen, but in a worst-case scenario, we need to be prepared. Keep in mind, it is Fashion Week, and besides the challenge of accommodations, every decent hair and makeup person is already booked. It's not like we had a year in advance to set this thing up."

Paige looks concerned.

"You'll be fine," I try to assure her.

"Does that mean I'll be doing Erin's hair and makeup too?" Paige is still acting a bit too much like a prima donna for me. I sure hope this isn't some kind of foreshadowing of what I can look forward to in the Big Apple.

"Good grief," I tell her. "It's not like I need to look *that* great. I'm only the camera girl and I go for a pretty natural look anyway. Relax, okay?"

"That's easy for you to say, *Camera Girl*, but I'm supposed to be the star and I need to look good. I can't show up at Fashion Week looking like something the cat dragged in."

Fran laughs. "Fine, I'll make a special note asking Leah to pay close attention to this one. Somehow we'll handle it, okay?"

"I hope so."

"And I get your point, Paige. If you don't look good we don't look good." Fran writes something down. "I'll be flying out with you and the three of us will share a suite that Leah managed to snag. As you can see on the schedule, Friday will be our day to acclimate ourselves to the city as well as do more strategizing. Then, first thing Saturday morning, the crew will be ready to hit the ground running. Or so we hope. Because, as you can see, that day is jammed—with less than a week before Fashion Week begins, design studios are hopping."

"I also see that we're scheduled to stay with Taylor Mitchell the following week. You're sure she's okay with that, right?" Paige asks.

"According to Leah, yes. It sounds like Taylor actually caught your last show and thinks highly of you, Paige."

Paige holds her head higher. "Hopefully she'll still feel that way when I meet her—I mean, if I have to do my own hair and makeup."

I try not to roll my eyes ... or yawn. Paige is so uptight. But I'll just chalk it up to nerves. A lot is riding on her during the next couple of weeks.

"I've got Helen Hudson on the line," Leah calls from her desk. "Want me to put her on speaker so she can talk to all of you?"

Fran turns on her speaker phone and we all listen as Helen wishes us a safe trip and success. "I'll fly in next Tuesday and attend the Perry Ellis show on Wednesday and then the Valentino on Friday," she says finally. "Now you girls be good and make me proud, you hear?"

We tell her we'll do our best and thank her before Fran hangs up. "So there you have it." She holds up her hands. "Since it's after six, I suggest you girls get home, finish packing, and get your beauty rest so that Paige doesn't end up looking like something the cat dragged in." She gives Paige a sly smile.

"By the way," Paige asks as we're leaving, "I assume we're flying first class, right?"

Fran just laughs. "Wrong. The best Leah could do was business class. Sorry about that."

Paige makes a pouty face. "How is it going to look if I get spotted flying business class?"

"Maybe you can disguise yourself," Fran teases. "Dark glasses, a scarf—go like an old-time Hollywood starlet."

Paige nods. "I just might do that."

Maybe I'm losing it, but the image of Paige playing a fifties movie starlet makes me laugh so hard that I actually snort.

"Attractive," Paige tells me as we're leaving.

"See you in the morning, girls," Fran calls out.

"Feeling nervous about the trip?" I ask Paige once we're in my Jeep. "You seemed a little edgy in there."

"Edgy?" She glances at me as I start the engine. "Why? What did I do?"

"Oh, you know, all that business about hair and makeup. Is it really that big of a deal?"

"It is to me. Seriously, Erin, our show is about looking good. How can I afford to go on the air without looking perfect?"

"Isn't that kind of hard to keep up all the time?"

Paige laughs. "Well, it does help that I'm fairly fabulous already."

"Not that you obsess over your looks or anything."

"My looks are what got us this job, Erin. I need to obsess a little."

I send up a quick prayer and tread carefully here. "But do you ever worry that you're just focusing on the outside, that you're maybe bordering on being ... superficial ... by worrying so much about appearances? I mean, what about what's underneath it all? What's left if you peel away the layers of fashion, makeup, even your natural good looks?"

Paige doesn't answer.

"What about your mind? Or even your heart?"

"What about them?" She holds up her hands in a helpless gesture. "They're there, aren't they? You're not suggesting I'm lacking those things, are you? I mean, it takes some brains and wit to do the interviews I do. And I have a heart, Erin. *Don't I?*" Her voice quivers ever so slightly and I wonder if I've hit a sore spot. I hope I haven't hurt her.

"Of course you do," I say quickly.

"I'm not you, I know," she says. "You seem to think it's enough to rely on your brains and ... well, maybe your faith. I'm not sure. But we're different, Erin. I can't be you. And you can't be me."

I laugh as I enter the freeway. "That's a good thing, isn't it."

She offers a small smile. "So maybe we should agree to disagree. You might think I'm all shallow and superficial and that I obsess over things like hair and makeup and fashion, but you don't have to pick on me for it, okay?"

"Okay." I nod vigorously. She's right. "I won't. And by the same token, maybe you should lay off picking on me for being unfashionable. Deal?"

"Well, I can pick on you a little," she says quickly. "You *are* on a TV show that's all about fashion. I can't just pretend you look great if you don't."

"Uh huh." I just shake my head. "Whatever."

"So how about this ..." She turns to look at me. "You are allowed to send me some kind of secret signal, okay?"

"Huh?"

"You know, like if you think I've stepped over the line ... or even if I'm about to step over some line."

"What kind of line?"

"You know, like I'm about to blast someone in the name

of honesty and fashion. I give you permission to tip me off if it looks like I'm going to seriously hurt someone, okay?"

"Okay." I feel myself brighten now. "What kind of secret signal will it be?"

"Good question."

We both sit there trying to come up with something, and after trying several we finally agree on the old throat-slash signal for *cut.*

"Since I'm not the one who ever tells you to cut, it should get your attention," I point out. "Plus the person you're interviewing will probably assume I'm just doing my job as camera girl." Hopefully it's not a signal I'll need to use much.

# Chapter 6

*"You girls have fun,"* Mom tells us as we're rushing to head out the door. It's not even six in the morning, and Mom's still in her bathrobe. But Fran just called saying that the limo is waiting, and we're scrambling to gather our stuff.

"I didn't know she was coming this early," I confess as I pull on my Ugg boots. "Our flight's not until nine-something."

"It was on the schedule," Paige yells as she comes rushing out of her room towing a very large pink suitcase behind her.

"Thanks to security right now, you're supposed to get to the airport two hours before your flight," Mom informs us. "And with morning commuter traffic, Fran's got it planned just about right."

"I'm going to have to make two trips," Paige complains, "just to get all this stuff downstairs." She groans as she heads out the door with her jumbo suitcase and matching carry-on bag.

"You'd think that the show hadn't already sent out boxes of clothes for us to wear," I say to Mom as I hug her. "Paige will have enough clothes to stay there permanently."

Mom laughs. "Just help keep an eye on her, okay? You know Paige doesn't always look before she leaps."

"I know. I'll do my best." I put the strap of my carry-on bag over my shoulder and pick up my roller bag. "Guess I'm ready to go now."

"Be careful, honey. And be sure to call me if you need anything," Mom says. "Or if you just need to talk."

"Thanks."

Mom looks a little forlorn as she waves.

"Enjoy the peace and quiet while we're gone," I tell her. "And make sure you call some friends and do something fun once in a while, okay?"

She nods, but her expression is still sad.

I meet Paige going up as I'm going down. "That's all you're taking?" she questions me.

I shrug. "I'm sure it's more than enough."

"Maybe for you." She rolls her eyes. "Some of us care about how we look."

"Yeah, yeah," I call as I go down. "I'll tell Fran you're coming ... and that you have like twelve more bags."

"Is that all you have?" Fran echos Paige after the driver takes my two bags and I hop into the back of the limo.

"I travel light."

"And you brought your camera too?"

"Of course."

"Wow, you do travel light."

"Well, the studio sent out clothes, right?" Suddenly I wonder if I dreamed that whole thing.

"Yes, of course."

"So I only need to bring clothes to wear when we're *not* doing the show, right?"

"Right."

"And according to that packed schedule, that's not a whole lot of time."

"Point taken."

Now Paige is clattering down the stairs with two more pink bags. "Besides," I tell Fran, "Paige will be using most of the plane's cargo space anyway."

Fran frowns. "I hope she knows that checked bags aren't free anymore."

"Do you think she'd even care?"

Paige surrenders the rest of her pink luggage to the driver, but when he can't fit the last bag into the trunk, he slides it into the back with us. "Looks like someone's moving away from home," he says to Paige with a twinkle in his eye.

"I just like having what I need with me," she says back.

"But do you really *need* all that?" Fran asks as he closes the door.

"You're the one who said I should be prepared to do hair and makeup. That alone took practically one whole bag."

"Oh, right." Fran nods. "Now you want to tell me what's up with all that pink?"

"Surely you know," I tease, "that all princesses travel with pink luggage. It's their trademark. In fact, I'm surprised that no rhinestones were harmed in the making of that luggage."

"Very funny." Paige scowls.

"She begged for that set of luggage for her fifteenth birthday." I try not to giggle. "Now she's stuck with it."

"I'm only stuck with it until I replace it with something more elegant," Paige confesses. "I've got my eye on a Burberry Brit set."

"In the meantime, you're the Pink Princess." I pretend to bow.

"You can mock me if you want, but there's actually a very sensible side to my pink luggage."

"Really?" Fran nods. "I'd like to hear this."

"Well, first of all, pink is easy to spot in baggage claim."

"Yes." Fran nods again. "That does make sense."

"But besides that, it's a security measure."

"Security?" Fran looks puzzled.

"I have a suspicion that most thieves would not want to be seen making off with my girlie pink luggage. Plus, if they try anything, it'd be very easy to pick them out of a crowd."

Fran chuckles. "Well, aren't you the sensible girl."

Paige smiles smugly. "Whereas your brown luggage and Erin's black luggage ... well, don't come crying to me if something goes missing."

"I don't know," I say. "I'm not sure I'd want to look like a pink princess just to make sure my clothes didn't get stolen."

"In your case, stolen clothes could be considered a good thing."

"Thanks a lot."

Fran is laughing. "You girls. Maybe we should try having a special sister spot on one of your shows, arguing like that. It could be highly entertaining."

"We could call it the sister spat spot," I offer.

But there's no time for spatting once we finally make it to the airport. Thanks to a wreck that shut the freeway down for more than an hour, we're already running late by the time we get to LAX. Fran has already called Leah to do what she can to get our flight changed, but just as we're being dropped off, Leah calls Fran to say she still hasn't found anything.

"We're going to have to run for it," Fran tells us as she dashes to snag a luggage cart for Paige to heap all her bags onto. "At least I thought to get our boarding passes online last night." She frowns at Paige, who's wheeling a small mountain of pink. "But it might take awhile to check those."

Somehow we get our bags checked and it actually looks like we might make it through security, but then Paige gets stopped because she stupidly packed a bottle of perfume in her carry-on.

And to make matters worse, she's about to throw a hissy fit when she's told it'll have to be disposed of. Fran is long gone now, already on her way to our gate, where she plans to beg the flight crew to wait. And I was ready to make a run for it too, but I can't just abandon my sister here. So I wait . . . and watch . . . and it's like I'm about to witness a train wreck.

"But it's Prada Infusion d'Iris," Paige protests. "It's brand new and it cost more than one hundred dollars."

"Too bad." The no-nonsense security guard sets the expensive Prada beside what appears to be a trash container.

"Wait! I can fit it into my Ziplock!" Paige is scrambling to open her already full Ziplock bag.

"Even if you *could* fit it into your Ziplock, it's more than three ounces," the woman tells her. "It has to go."

"But what if I empty some of the perfume out?" Paige smiles hopefully. "Or I could use some. Look, it's only three point four ounces. I could use up point four ounces."

I look at my watch and know we don't have time for this. "Just let it go," I yell at her. "And come on!"

Just then, Paige reaches over and takes the perfume bottle, and I'm thinking *bad move, Paige.* Really, really bad move. I give my sister the slash-throat *cut* sign, thinking maybe she'll get a clue and stop this craziness. But she's not looking my way. So I just stare helplessly as the scene unfolds — it seems almost like it's in slow motion. Paige has her precious perfume in one hand, Ziplock in the other. She's trying to open the perfume. And the middle-aged, overweight female security guard is glaring at her as she says something into the Bluetooth wired to her head. Most likely calling for backup.

Paige is totally oblivious to the guard as she liberally squirts perfume on herself like she thinks she's really going to use up nearly half an ounce. And then with a playful expression — maybe she imagines she's a department store fragrance sales-girl — she looks like she's actually planning to spray perfume on the security guard as well. Before Paige gets the chance, two uniformed guys swoop out of nowhere and my sister is literally tackled and, just like that, they pin her flat on the filthy airport floor. One guy, with his knee in the center of her back, cuffs her hands behind her as if she's a dangerous criminal.

Paige is screaming at them to stop, but it's like they can't even hear her or maybe they just don't care. And, although I'm stunned at how dumb she was — not to mention an out-of-contral diva — I can't help but feel this is a bit much.

"*Stop it!*" I yell at them, finally finding my voice, as I fumble for my phone. "Leave her alone!" With shaking fingers I hit Fran's number, watching as my sister remains pinned to the dirty floor. "Fran!" I cry when she finally answers. "Paige is being mugged!"

"Mugged?" Fran shoots back.

"By security!" Then I describe the scene and Fran lets loose with some colorful language.

"I'm on my way," she tells me. "Stay with Paige!"

"And call my mom," I yell back at her.

"Just stay calm," she warns me. "Whatever you do, *stay calm*."

I keep this in mind as I approach the female security guard. *Stay calm.* "That's my sister there on the floor," I tell her. "Why are they—"

"Code four," the woman says into her Bluetooth while looking warily at me. "APT at SG twenty-one."

"But I'm not doing any—"

The next thing I know, I too am grabbed from behind, but thankfully I'm not thrown to the ground. Even so their treatment of me is unnecessarily rough, especially considering I've done nothing wrong, and I'll bet I'm going to have bruises to show for this little skirmish. Then, like Paige, I'm handcuffed. The nylon bands are so tight that my fingers start to feel numb.

"It's going to be okay," I tell Paige. "I called Fran and she's going to call Mom." I glance at the security guard woman and try another tactic. "My mom is a producer at Channel Five News and, trust me, this mistreatment will make tonight's edition if you don't put a stop to it."

She says something else in code into her Bluetooth and I decide to continue trying to talk sense into this woman. "I know my sister didn't handle this right. But I also saw how she was assaulted and knocked down," I say calmly. "And you may not care that she's a celebrity with her own TV show, but I know her fans will also be interested to hear about this kind of treatment."

The woman looks a tiny bit worried and I'm feeling hopeful. "I know it was wrong of her to act like that about her perfume, but—"

"*Be quiet*," the woman hisses at me.

"Get these girls out of here," one of the other guards commands.

And suddenly two guys are flanking me and I'm being firmly escorted away. I glance over my shoulder to see that Paige is on her feet now and she too is being escorted away—but in a different direction. Her face is so pale it doesn't even look like her, and I wonder *how is this possible?* All this nonsense over a silly bottle of perfume.

Even though I know Paige was really dumb to do what she did, these security guards are acting more like out-of-control thugs. And that's exactly what I tell the other security people when I'm brought to their office for what feels like an interrogation. After my shakedown, I also tell them about my mom being a news producer and that she's probably bringing our lawyer as well as Channel Five cameras. Not that anyone seems to listen or care. Maybe they think I'm making this stuff up. Finally, I just shut my mouth and silently pray for help.

Finally, a woman who introduces herself as Donna comes in. "We're sorry for your inconvenience, Miss Forrester," she says after my handcuffs have been removed and I'm attempting to rub the feeling and the blood back into my fingers. "Obviously, you are not a threat to security. But we do need to be careful."

"Your guards *should* be more careful." I hold up my hands to show Donna the red welts those horrid handcuffs cut into my wrists. "They could seriously injure someone."

"Our guards are trained to deal with criminals and terrorists," she says as she sets aside my ticket and boarding pass, and returns the contents of my wallet back to me. Meanwhile another guard has finished ransacking my carry-on bag. He opened everything and took it all apart and even examined my camera like he thought I was trying to smuggle state secrets in it. Perhaps he thought that is was really a homemade bomb. I wonder if Paige is going through the same kind of interrogation ... and how she's holding up.

"But I'm not a criminal or a terrorist," I say for the umpteenth time. "And neither is my sister."

"I think we have almost established that, Miss Forrester, but we take all security risks equally seriously. It's for your safety as much as for anyone else's. And when your sister threatened the guard—"

"Threatened the guard?" I question. "With *perfume*?"

"The guard had no way of knowing what was in that bottle. And when a passenger acts questionably like that, our guards are trained to think fast and act swiftly. For all our guard knew there could've been something toxic or explosive in that bottle."

"But there wasn't. And my sister squirted herself with it first. That should've proved it wasn't dangerous. And I could smell it clear over to where I was standing. It was obviously perfume!"

"We'll get to the bottom of it," Donna assures me. She's now checking my phone, writing down the numbers stored there like maybe my friends and family are cohorts in crime, or fellow spies, or crazed terrorists. And even when my phone rings, she doesn't let me answer it.

"We're going to miss our flight," I say hopelessly. Like I even care at the moment. Right now, I'm mostly just worried about Paige.

"There are other flights to New York," she says calmly.

But as I sit there, replaying this whole weird incident through my head, I'm thinking this is seriously twisted. I mean, I care as much as anyone about safety and preventing terrorist attacks, but to tackle a young woman for squirting perfume, then to hold us long enough to miss our plane, to be treated like criminals ... And I wonder if what they've done is even legal.

# Chapter 7

*After about thirty minutes of being impris-*oned in this stuffy airport office, my things are finally returned to me. I repack my bag and am released—just like that. I guess they can't keep holding you if you haven't done anything wrong. Still, I wonder if I should talk to a lawyer. And, as I go through security and then wander down the terminal, I can't help but wonder if this all might just be a bad dream. Maybe I haven't even gotten out of bed yet. But my ringing phone jars me back to reality. To my relief, it's Mom. I tell her I'm okay, then ask about Paige.

"She's not with you?"

"No. I was being questioned by security. They treated me like a terrorist and—"

"I know. But we'll discuss that later. Right now we need to find your sister."

"Totally. What should I do?"

"Call Fran. She's still over there, on the other side of the security gates, trying to find where they've taken Paige. We'd hoped you two girls were together. I've arrived at the airport, but I can't get through security without a boarding pass. But I do have someone over here trying to help me sort this nonsense out."

"Right." I cautiously walk back toward the security gates. I seriously do not want to get too close to those freaks again. Who knows what they might do next?

"The reason I was so concerned for you girls is that we've done some news stories on this very thing," Mom explains. "I know some security agents can be pretty rough. And I'm worried about Paige."

"I am too."

"Oh, I need to go," Mom says quickly. "I think they've located Paige. I'll call you right back as soon as I know something for sure. But you find Fran and stay with her in the meantime, okay?"

"Okay." And just as I hang up, I spot Fran pacing near the security area with an anxious expression and her phone to her ear. I wave, then hurry over and throw my arms around her like a long-lost friend.

"This is so crazy," I say. "I feel like I'm a stranger in some foreign country, like I might be thrown into prison if I don't watch my step."

"I'm so sorry, Erin," Fran says. "Any news on Paige?"

"Mom said she thought someone found her. She's going to call back as soon as she knows."

"This is just outrageous." Fran shakes her head. "I was just talking to Helen and she's having a total fit. She's already called her attorney and I know your mother has some of her news crew here. I think we should make this story as big as possible."

"I just hope, for Paige's sake, it's not too big since she's partly to blame for this." Just then my phone rings. Mom tells me that Paige is being released and explains where Fran and I should go to meet up with her.

"I'll call you the minute we find her," I promise.

"And then come out here," Mom tells me. "We're going to get this story while it's still fresh and we'll run it on the news tonight. This is something every traveler needs to hear."

Soon we're reunited with Paige near the security gate, and she literally looks like "what the cat dragged in." I hug her and ask if she's okay.

"Okay?" she says quietly. "You must be joking."

"Mom's here," I tell her as I hit speed dial for my mom's cell phone. "Paige is with us," I tell Mom.

"Great, now you girls hurry on over here." Mom tells me where to meet them and I tell Paige about Mom's plan to put this on the news.

"Channel Five News?" Paige's expression is hard to read, but she doesn't look happy. "What about New York?"

"Well, we've obviously missed that flight," Fran tells her. "But I've spoken to the airline and they're booking us for a later one."

"Mom's got a news team here with her," I continue telling Paige as Fran and I exit past security. I try not to glare at the guards as we pass, but they seem preoccupied anyway. Probably waiting to mug some little old lady.

"Anyway, your mom wants to make this a story," Fran explains. "A big story! And that means free publicity for us."

"I don't know..." Paige's eyes look frightened and her mascara has run clear down her cheeks. I'm sure she has no idea how bedraggled she looks.

"People need to hear about how you were treated," I tell her. "Are you okay with that?"

Paige puts her hand to her left cheek. It's dirty and swollen and has what looks like the beginning of a good-sized bruise, probably from when she was shoved to the floor. "I guess so … maybe I should go clean up first," she says in a shaky voice.

"Just a little," Fran exchanges a concerned glance with me then points toward a nearby restroom.

We go over to the sink area and Paige gasps to see herself. Using wet paper towels and tissues, combined with the limited beauty products Fran and I can come up with between us—a necessity since it seems security kept all that was in Paige's Ziplock bag—we do our best to help Paige pull herself together. And even when she looks pretty good, she seems close to tears.

"Are you sure you can do this?" I ask her.

"Do what?" She gives me a blank look.

"The news story. Mom will understand if you're too—"

"No." Now Paige tosses a wadded paper towel into the trash and stands up straight. "I need to tell this story. People have a right to know."

As we hurry back to the ticketing area, I silently pray for Paige. I ask God to help her to be strong. And I ask him to use this whole thing—what seems like a nightmare—and to bring something good from it.

Before long, we are set up and ready to shoot. A small crowd of onlookers is gathering and then cameras (including mine) are rolling. "I'm Susan Sanders from Channel Five News," the reporter begins, "and we are live at Los Angeles International Airport, one of the busiest air terminals in the world, where just minutes ago, Paige Forrester, star of *On the Runway*, endured a horrifying experience with airport security. Can you tell us what happened?"

And so Paige begins to recount the story, how we were on our way to New York for Fashion Week, how we were running late and just going through security. "It didn't seem like a big deal at first," she says, "and I'll admit that I was at fault for forgetting to remove a small bottle of perfume from my carry-on. I had stuck it in at the last minute and had meant to transfer it to a checked bag, but we were in a rush." She goes on to tell about how she wanted to use up enough to make it less than three ounces and how she was tackled. "After that, I was kind of in shock. I mean, one minute you're standing there just laughing and joking and the next thing you know two big guys have knocked you down and pinned you to the ground." She touches her cheek where the swelling is still visible.

"So they actually tackled you?" Susan asks, "Just because you squirted perfume on yourself?"

Paige nods with sad eyes. "And it's a nice fragrance too. Prada Infusion d'Iris, and not cheap either."

Susan laughs. "Tell us what happened next."

"They handcuffed my wrists behind my back, so tightly that my fingers got numb. And it seemed like they kept me pinned on the ground for a long time, and this guy had his knee in my back like I was going to get up and run. Finally, they took me to a security office." Paige stops now.

"And what happened there?"

Paige takes in a slow breath. "I was totally humiliated in a strip search."

"A strip search?" Susan's eyes grow wide. "With the male security guards?"

"No, two women did that, actually. But the guys weren't far away, and for all I know they might've been watching. It was horrid and humiliating and disgusting and no one should have to suffer like that. Not for squirting themselves with perfume anyway. I mean, I can admit that I wasn't being too smart. But they took this too far. Way too far."

"So what happened after they strip-searched you?"

"They made me wear this creepy paper robe thing, kind of like in the doctor's office. And then they went through all my clothes, as if I had something hidden in there. And they went through my carry-on bag and my purse, just pulled everything apart. I never even got all my things back."

"They kept some of your things?"

"I don't know if was intentional or not. When they told me I could go, I just grabbed everything—as fast as I could—and ran out of there."

"It sounds traumatizing."

Paige nods. "I've never been through anything so dehumanizing before. And all because of some silly perfume."

"That does seem very extreme."

"And my sister was arrested and taken into custody too," Paige continues. "And she didn't do anything. She was just telling them to quit hurting me."

So now I get pulled into this. But for Paige's sake, I do my best. "That's right," I say when Susan holds a hand mic to my face. "I didn't do anything wrong. And suddenly I was handcuffed." I hold up my wrists, which are still red. "It hurts where they cut into my skin. Then I was questioned and my bags were thoroughly searched."

"Were you strip-searched as well?"

"No. Thank goodness. I think I might've totally lost it if that had happened. I don't know how Paige could've stood being treated like that."

Susan asks Paige a few more questions then begins to

recount other incidents of passengers who've been treated like this. "Fortunately, this hasn't been a common experience at LAX. But it is happening more often than it should, and although few people can be prepared for this when it does happen, you need to know you have rights. A number of victims of security abuse are taking legal action. I have spoken to Paige and Erin's mother, and she informed me that attorneys are already looking into this."

She wraps the story up by asking about our plans for New York. Paige makes a magnificent recovery as she talks about our new show and how *On the Runway* will be covering a variety of fashion-related events in the Big Apple. She even manages to mention the day and time that our show airs.

"And hopefully, you won't have anymore unfortunate incidents like you experienced here at LAX this morning. But travelers beware—the application of perfume in security could put a serious damper on your next vacation. This is Susan Sanders for Channel Five News."

"This will run on *Midday Report*," Mom assures us after the cameras shut down. "And again tonight."

"Great," Fran says. "And now if we hurry over to the ticket counter, we might be able to make the twelve fifteen *direct* flight to LaGuardia."

Mom hugs us and tells us to be careful. "And our cameras are going to follow you right up to the security gates," she says, "and they will be filming until you get through just in case something happens again."

"I can't imagine they'd dare anything like that," Fran assures her.

Before long, we have direct first class tickets to New York. But as we—and our entourage—approach security, I can tell

Paige is getting nervous. "Okay," I tell her. "You don't have any fluids on you, right?"

"Are you kidding?" She shakes her head. "They confiscated everything."

"Now, you'll just calmly remove your shoes and your jacket," I remind her. Between Fran and me, we somehow coach Paige through security without any further ado. In fact, every single security person is polite and gracious and I have to wonder why it couldn't have gone down like that the first time. Still, I'm thankful the grumpy female security guard is nowhere to be seen. I can only hope that she and the others are being repremanded.

We have an hour to wait at our gate, but we use this time to forage for food. All three of us are ravenous after our exhausting morning. And then I go with Paige to stock up on fashion magazines, and even pretend like I'm into it for once. Anything to cheer her up. Just as we're being loaded in the first boarding group, Fran's phone rings. As we're getting into our seats, which are nice comfy leather recliners, we can hear Fran across the aisle talking. I'm guessing it's Helen, and it must be something upbeat because Fran is grinning from ear to ear.

"Guess what, girls?" she asks after she hangs up.

"Those nasty airport security thugs are being strip-searched by gorillas?" I try.

Paige chuckles. "I wish."

"This is almost as good," Fran says quickly. "Helen says that she's heard from a reliable source that your news story is likely to be picked up nationally, and she's already contacted a producer friend at *Good Morning America* who would like you girls to be on their show tomorrow."

"To talk about *On the Runway*?" Paige looks hopeful.

"No, to talk about the airport security incident. But I'm sure you can somehow get a few words in for our show as well. And it's a great opportunity, don't you think?"

It's hard to read Paige's face. I know the girl loves publicity, but I suspect she's not overly eager to tell the strip-search story too many times. Although I suppose it could end up being therapeutic.

"And who knows?" Fran continues. "If the GMA interview goes well ... maybe *Today* will call. Or maybe GMA will want to invite you back next week to talk about *On the Runway* at Fashion Week."

"I guess we should make the most of it." Paige nods. "Besides, it might actually help some other unsuspecting girl to not make the same mistake."

"By the way," Fran adds. "Helen said that Prada is probably sending you a little something as a consolation gift. We'll check with the concierge at the hotel tomorrow."

Paige doesn't even respond as she opens a thick edition of *Vogue*. "You know, I'd just like to forget about the whole thing ... for a while."

"Me too," I agree.

Paige leans back into the seat with a contented expression. "First class is definitely the way to go."

"That was so cool that the airline upgraded us," I tell her. "I mean, it's not like they were responsible for the security people."

"But what a price to pay." Paige sighs.

"I'll say." I slowly shake my head. Then I peer curiously at my sister, suddenly wondering if she might've intentionally pulled that whole crazy stunt just to get ... No, that is way too extreme. Even for a drama queen like Paige. But it just figures that she would end up with a payoff like this. My sister sometimes takes a beating, but she usually lands on her feet.

"So what time do we get in to New York?" I ask Fran.

"We probably won't get settled in our hotel until nearly midnight," she says.

"Midnight?" Paige looks surprised. "And what time do we have to get up for *Good Morning America*?"

"They want us in the studio by six thirty."

Paige does not look pleased. "So that's like three in the morning West Coast time?"

"Yes, but you shouldn't think about it like that," Fran warns. "Set your clock on Eastern time and just forget—"

"So I'll be getting a few hours' sleep, if I'm lucky, and at three in the morning I have to show up at *Good Morning America* looking fresh and pretty and fashionable and chic?"

"Fashionable and chic, always." Fran nods. "Fresh and pretty ...? Well, let's just settle for a worn-out sort of pretty. Everyone will know you've been through an ordeal."

"Don't worry," I assure Paige. "By tomorrow, you'll be looking gorgeous again." *And*, I think to myself, *I'll be looking for a camera to hide behind.*

# Chapter 8

After a relatively pleasant and un-eventful flight, it's about eleven when we finally make our way to baggage claim in LaGuardia. Our internal clocks still seem to be on Pacific time, where it's only eight, so we chatter amongst ourselves as we wait for the luggage near the airport office, where our bags would be stored because of the earlier flight. But then we wait and wait and wait ... and you'd think that our luggage would be easy to find with all of Paige's pink bags, but after about twenty minutes we realize we have a problem.

Fortunately, Fran is on top of it. She's already notified a man who is trying to track down the whereabouts of our bags. "It sounds like they're stowed somewhere else, and if we stick around we can just take them with us instead of waiting for someone from the airline to deliver them to the hotel."

"I'll feel better waiting," Paige tells her. "Especially with *Good Morning America* in the morning. All my hair accessories and cosmetics are in a checked bag."

But after nearly an hour, we are worried and antsy. "What

if they *really* lost our bags?" I ask Fran after she informs us that they weren't on our original New York flight.

"They *have* lost our bags, Erin," Paige says impatiently. "Aren't you listening?"

"I mean lost them *for good.*"

Suddenly Paige looks like she's about to cry or maybe just scream uncontrollably. And I realize I'd better not push this girl's buttons.

"The bags have to be somewhere," Fran reassures us. "And Paige's pink luggage would be hard to misplace — for long anyway. I'm sure they'll be at our hotel by morning."

"Yes," I say quickly. "So maybe that's where we should be too."

Fran points over to where our limo is still waiting. "Let's blow this joint."

"Watch what you say," I tell her. "Security might be listening."

Fran laughs as we hurry to the limo, but once we're inside, it's clear to see that Paige is not handling this well. In fact, she looks close to a meltdown.

"Are you okay?" I quietly ask.

Her lips are pressed tightly together, and it could be my imagination, but it looks like her nostrils are flared. "How do you think I am?"

I just shrug and glance nervously at Fran. I know my sister, and there are a few specific (seemingly minor) things that can totally unravel her otherwise unflappable personality. Things like: One, being humiliated in public; two, being observed by almost anyone when she's not looking "picture perfect"; and three, losing her stuff. Right now I'm worried that we're facing the triple threat.

"How do you think I am?" she repeats with a snarl.

"You've had a rough day. I know."

"But you're in New York City," Fran says pleasantly as she points out the window of the limo. "Just look at those lights — this is the city that — "

"I am in the fashion capital of the United States," Paige says in a monotone, "and my cosmetics and my hair products and even my clothes are all MIA. I am supposed to appear on national TV in — " she glances at her watch. "In about six hours. I will not be able to sleep. I have a bruised face. My hair is totally gross. My clothes are — "

"The clothes from the studio should be in our hotel," Fran says quickly.

"Yes, that's just fine," Paige shoots back at her. "I'll be dressed for the runway but I will look like I've been run over." And then she starts crying.

I wish I could think of something to say, but I feel over my head.

"We'll go to ABC early," Fran tells her. "I'll find you hair and makeup stylists and you'll look fine."

Paige blots her tears with a tissue. "Thanks. We'll see what they can do with my puffy eyes," she says with a sniff.

"You'll look fine," I assure her. "I've never seen anyone who can recover and pull herself together faster than you, Paige. And besides, you shouldn't look too perfect tomorrow — "

"You mean today," she corrects me.

"Yes. Today. You should look a little bedraggled. I mean, you're going on their show to talk about the ordeal you went through with security. If you look perfect, they might not believe you."

"That's right," Fran agrees. "You want to win the public's

sympathy. Otherwise, you'll look like a spoiled fashion princess who goes around complaining about everything."

Paige seems to be considering this, and I think maybe we just averted a total meltdown. And yet I realize we're not home free yet. As we get out of the limo and head into the hotel, I feel like I'm transporting volatile explosives, and like I should warn everyone (including helpful doormen) to just back off Paige so nobody gets hurt.

Fran gets us checked in, and then as Paige gazes at a window display of some elegant beauty products that are available at the spa/salon (when it's open), Fran quietly gives me the key card and tells me to take my sister up to the suite. "Just get her to take a relaxing bath before bed." Fran reaches into her bag now, pulling out a small pill bottle. "And, if you need to, give her one of these."

"What is it?"

"Just a very mild sleeping pill. Right now, I think Paige could use one. In the meantime, I'll check with the concierge about the clothes the studio shipped and I'll see if he can send someone out to procure some beauty products—things Paige will need if her bag doesn't make it. Why don't you ask her what exactly she needs and call me back with a list?"

I'm not so sure about this plan, or whether or not Paige should take a sleeping pill, but I pocket the bottle and pry Paige away from the display case before she attempts to break in and snatch the beauty products.

Our two-bedroom suite turns out to be just that. *Sweet.* But Paige doesn't seem to even notice the cool contemporary furnishings, big windows, or even the luxurious amenities, like a cashmere throw at the foot of the bed. Cashmere! But I have a feeling that nothing is going to impress this girl tonight. "You get undressed," I say as I hand her a fluffy white terry robe. "I'll run you a bath."

She just nods. "Thanks."

I pour some fragrant-smelling bath product into the elegant tub and run the water, making sure that it's nice and warm but not boiling hot. And before long Paige is settled down into the bubbles and giving me her wish list of hair and beauty products. While she's soaking, I call Fran and relay this list to her.

"I just got a kit of basic personal products from the hotel," Fran tells me. "I'll give Paige's list to the concierge and hope for the best. Is Paige in bed yet?"

"She's just getting out of the tub," I say, feeling more like a mommy than a younger sister. "I'm loaning her a T-shirt from my carry-on to use to sleep in."

"Well, give her one of those pills and tuck her in and kiss her good night, Erin. That girl really needs some beauty sleep. And she'll be lucky to get four hours at this rate."

So I show Paige the bottle of sleep-aid pills. "Fran thinks you should take one of these," I tell her.

"Good idea." She reaches for the bottle and I retrieve an Evian from the mini bar and hand it to her. And before I can repeat "just one pill," Paige pops two into her mouth and washes them down. "What's wrong?" she asks me.

I just shrug and hope that two pills aren't too much. Not that there's anything I can do about that now. "You better get to bed," I say as I take back the pill bottle. "Just try to relax and don't worry about the morning. Fran and I will wake you up and you'll be fine."

She nods and then smiles. "Thanks, Erin. I couldn't do this without you."

"Just rest, okay?" Then I turn out the light and grab a quick shower. By the time I'm done, Fran is back.

"They're sending the boxes from the studio up. I asked if they could have someone press them in time for morning, but that's not going to happen this late at night." She glances over to a closet. "Do you suppose there's an ironing board in here?"

I hunt around until I find one in the bedroom closet. I make a fair amount of noise pulling it out, but Paige seems to be sound asleep. Then I remember the sleeping pills. After I'm back out into the main part of the suite, I tell Fran about Paige taking two pills.

"You let her take two?"

"I didn't *let* her. I told her one and then she took two."

Fran frowns.

"Is this going to be a problem?" I ask, anxious.

"Let's hope not. But just in case, make sure that coffee pot is in the kitchen ready to go in the morning. I'll set my alarm for five thirty."

As I'm setting up the coffee pot, the boxes from the studio arrive and, while Fran's taking a shower, I unpack the boxes and just start in on the ironing. Does it strike me as odd that my first night in the Big Apple is spent waiting on my sister and ironing clothes at three in the morning? Maybe. Or maybe some people are just designed to be caretakers ... and others are just designed to need caretaking. Anyway, it doesn't really bother me. Much. Mostly I just want Paige to be ready to pull off the morning show without any more unnecessary stress to her or to me.

It's nearly four when I finish ironing. I pressed more clothes than needed, but I wasn't sure what Paige would want to wear and I was trying to cover my bases. I already told Fran to get some rest, and I'm just thinking about grabbing a nap too when I hear a quiet knock at the door. I look out the peephole to see it's a bellboy holding a large Walgreens bag.

"Thanks," I tell him as I take the bag. But he just stands there and I realize he wants a tip. "Just a sec." I close the door and run for my purse, digging until I find a couple of rumpled ones and wonder if that's enough. But I'm not about to give him a ten.

"Sorry, this is all I can spare right now," I tell him. He just nods and mumbles "thanks" in a way that suggests he's as uncomfortable with this little setup as I am. And I wish I'd had a five—or perhaps been generous enough to give him the ten. Maybe next time.

I open the bag and am surprised to see that he's managed to get a number of the items on Paige's list. I'm thinking she should be relatively pleased. Of course, some of the products are obviously substitutions and I'm sure she'll consider them substandard. But you never know. Even in the area of beauty, I suppose that desperate times might call for desperate measures.

I arrange these things in the bathroom. Finally, I'm ready to get a little sleep, but I am not sleepy. After tossing and turning for half an hour, I get out of bed and go to the living room to watch TV. In less than an hour it'll be time to get up anyway.

I'm just finishing up *M*A*S*H* when I hear an alarm ringing in Fran's room. And just when I was getting sleepy too. But I get up and turn on the coffee pot, then go to wake up Paige.

"Time to get up, Sleeping Beauty," I tell her.

But she's totally out, flopped over on one side and snoring.

I gently shake her shoulder, but it's no use. "Paige," I urge, "you need to wake up for *Good Morning America*. Remember?"

"She's not up yet?" Fran asks sleepily as she walks in the room.

"Those two sleeping pills must've worked."

"They can't have worked this well. You pour her some coffee and I'll get a cold washcloth."

By the time I get back with the coffee, Paige is sitting on the edge of her bed with a frown. My T-shirt is all rumpled and twisted and her face has the creases of sleep marks on it, probably wrinkles from the pillowcase. To make matters worse, her swollen cheek is now starting to darken with a bruise. Lovely. I control the urge to run and cover the mirrors with sheets. "Here, Paige," I tell her as I hand her the coffee. "Careful, it's hot."

She nods and takes the cup but doesn't drink.

"Come on," Fran urges her, "just drink a little."

Paige sleepily lifts the cup to her mouth, but she's not very focused and before it gets to her lips, she tips it and the next thing I know scalding hot coffee is pouring down her neck and chin and she jumps up screaming and swearing and tearing off the wet T-shirt.

"That's one way to wake her up," Fran tells me with a hint of a smile.

I grab up the wet washcloth and hand it to Paige. "Here, put this on your chin and then jump into the shower."

I run ahead and turn the shower on, adjusting it to a cool (not cold) temperature, and I practically shove Paige in. Again she screams and I wonder if hotel security is on its way up to see if we're murdering someone.

"It's freezing," she cries.

"That's okay," I yell back. "It'll help the burn. Just run it cool for a bit and then you can wash your hair."

"I'm going to put together an outfit for her," Fran calls out.

I run to get the shampoo and conditioner—Paige's favorite brand—and run back and hand them to her. "Look," I say triumphantly. "The bellboy brought these up last night. I think he raided the hotel's salon."

She grumbles thank you and I hang a couple of towels as well as her bathrobe within easy reach. Then I rush out and grab up the telephone and call for room service. "Can we get yogurt and pastries and some orange juice and maybe some kind of fresh berries up here ... really fast?" I ask the woman. "It's kind of an emergency."

"Emergency?" the woman questions.

"Yes," I say urgently. "Low blood sugar." Okay, this isn't completely true.

"Oh, yes, yes, of course," she says quickly. "We'll get that to you right away."

I thank her and hang up.

"Paige has low blood sugar?" Fran asks with concern.

I make a sheepish smile. "Not exactly. But Mom and I have this theory about her. Ever since she was a little girl, we noticed that she can be seriously cantankerous when she's hungry. Unfortunately, she doesn't always realize it until it's too late. And sometimes she skips meals because she gets the crazy idea that she's fat. Anyway, I figured I'd better plan ahead. Just in case."

"Smart thinking." Fran winks at me. "I can see more and more why Helen had the foresight to put you on the team."

I want to say something snarky like "you must mean the B string." And yet, I'm not sure I really care so much anymore.

I used to care. It used to hurt that Paige was in the limelight while I was stuck in the back, making sure the generator was still running. Now I'm not so sure. It seems that being the front-runner comes with its own set of pressures and stress. I feel thankful not to have to deal with that.

# Chapter
## 9

*I'm just returning from the bathroom where* I encouraged Paige to drink (not absorb) a cup of coffee that I set in front of her. She had been just standing there like a zombie, staring blankly at the mirror. I wonder if she needs something stronger than caffeine to shake the effect of those sleeping pills.

Fran is still sorting through the clothes that I ironed and hung last night. She holds up a pale blue jacket and skirt. (Chanel, as I recall, which I think is supposed to be pretty impressive.) "What do you think?"

I frown slightly. "It's really nice. But it just doesn't quite scream Paige Forrester to me. I think it's too serious for her."

"I meant for you, silly."

I just shrug. "Yeah, sure." I want to tell her that I'd rather be wearing my camera girl outfit and hanging back behind the scenes, but I suspect that she, like me, is fed up with drama this morning.

"You go use my bathroom," she says as she hands me the suit and some shoes and things. "Get dressed and ready and

I'll deal with Paige. And put on some makeup too, Erin. You look really washed out. Some blush and lip color, *okay*?"

"Okay."

It feels kind of surreal as I'm getting ready. Maybe it's lack of sleep, or jet lag, or being a strange place, or whatever. But I go through the paces, doing as Fran told me, putting on makeup the way that Paige has shown me. I'm just finishing up and thinking I didn't do too badly when I hear someone at the door. Thankfully, it's room service.

"Oh, good," Fran says as she emerges from the bathroom, where I can hear Paige complaining loudly about something. "We could desperately use that food right now."

Fran takes care of the bill and I go to check on Paige. But as soon as I see her, I can tell all is not well. Her hair, though dry, looks strangely limp and stringy and slightly greasy. Her left cheek is swollen and the bruise is somewhat camouflaged by makeup, but the total effect isn't exactly right. Like maybe she has jaundice or something.

"Look at my hair," she cries. "It's ruined."

"What happened?"

"That stupid shampoo and conditioner!" She glares at me as she picks up her lip liner and attempts to line her lips, although she seems to be coloring outside of the lines today.

"But it's your brand, Paige, and it was—"

"The wrong formula. In case you haven't noticed. I don't need extra conditioning to tame my natural curl. Anyone can see that I need the sleek, shiny, bouncy formula."

"Oh ..." And the truth is, I *can* see. She needs it and she needs it now.

She points to her face. "And this foundation is so wrong."

"Maybe you can change it at the ABC studio," I suggest.

"That's what Fran promised."

"And Fran wants you to drink this." Fran says as she hands Paige a glass of orange juice.

So, in between shoving food at her and trying to improve her appearance, which is a challenge, Fran and I take turns at keeping Paige (who is still sluggish) moving in the right direction.

"Do you think we should just cancel?" I ask Fran quietly as we wait for Paige to finish her mascara, which is looking kind of smudgy and scary.

Fran just shakes her head. "You know what they say about publicity."

"Any publicity is good publicity," I repeat without conviction.

"And besides," Fran brightens, "we still have you. If all else fails, you better be ready to jump in and take over for Zombie Girl."

I feel myself getting ready to argue and balk, but then I remind myself I'm here in New York not as a tourist, which sounds like fun, but as an employee. It's not like I can refuse to work.

"Fortunately we're less than a mile from the studio," Fran says as she's ushering Paige from the bathroom. "And there should be a car down there waiting for us."

As we're getting ready to leave, Paige picks up a piece of pastry from the room service tray. She begins munching on it and is totally oblivious to the fact that it's crumbling down the front of her black-and-white Michael Kors dress. But I fig-ure this is something we can straighten up later—when we're straightening up everything else (like her hair and makeup, which even I can see look pretty bad). As Fran gathers her bag and things, Paige leans against the doorway with drooping eyelids and I'm tempted to grab another cup of coffee, thinking she can drink as we ride, but images of Paige wearing coffee stains on top of her Danish crumbs stops me.

"I'm going to meet *Diane Sawyer*," Paige says in a dreamy voice as she crosses her legs and leans back in the town car.

"Well, I'm not sure who'll be interviewing," Fran admits as she checks her BlackBerry.

As our car slowly inches down the jammed avenue, Paige closes her eyes and I suspect she's actually sleeping. Honestly, I think we could probably walk faster. But about twenty minutes later than planned, we are finally at the studio.

After waiting several more minutes, we're met by a girl named Cleo. She has us sign some release forms, gives us a short tour, and finally takes us to the greenroom.

"But what about makeup and hair?" I quietly ask Cleo as Paige sits down in what looks like a far-too-comfortable overstuffed chair.

"Oh, there's no time for that," she informs me, glancing at her clipboard. "You girls are going on in exactly nineteen minutes."

Fortunately, Paige now seems oblivious (thanks to her sleepiness) about her appearance. And equally fortunately, there isn't a mirror in this room. So I'm hoping maybe we can get through this without too much ado. Besides, I tell myself, the interview will probably take all of three minutes, five minutes tops. TV always changes the way you look anyway. And Paige is a very photogenic girl. Usually, anyway. I glance uncomfortably at Fran now. She's frowning at Paige, who has her head leaning back and looks as if she's about to start snoring again.

"What exactly were in those pills anyway?" I hiss at Fran.

"Never mind that," she hisses back. "We need to fix her up more."

So Fran and I use what little we can find in Fran's bag, doing our best to make Paige look like Paige. But it seems a losing battle. Sure, we fix her smudged mascara and sloppy lip lines, but she just doesn't look like herself. Perhaps more worrisome is that she's not acting like herself. Even as the sound guy is helping us to get wired, I feel like I need to explain to him that, really, Paige has not been drinking.

"Time to head out," Cleo comes in to tell us. She peers curiously at Paige, who still looks barely awake. "Is she okay?"

"Yesterday was pretty stressful for her," I tell Cleo as we head down the hallway.

"That's right." Paige nods sleepily. "I'm not over it."

"Robin Roberts will be doing your interview," Cleo says as she reaches for the door. "Time to be quiet now."

Paige frowns. "Not Diane?"

"I really like Robin Roberts," I whisper quickly. "She's cool."

With her hand still on the door, Cleo looks questionably at Paige. "Now they're getting ready to break. You girls know how to do this, right?"

"Absolutely," I assure her.

"Three, two, one," she whispers as she opens the door.

And suddenly we're being escorted out to the chairs where Robin is standing off to one side talking to a producer and going over her notes. Paige is set up in the chair which I assume will be opposite Robin's and I sit next to Paige. As the break continues, I silently pray. It seems like an unusually long break—or else it's just nerves—but suddenly they're doing a countdown and just like that, Robin slips into her chair with a bright smile directed at the camera. She focuses on the teleprompter and launches into a monologue about airport security and the need for it.

"But sometimes security goes too far. And when a young lady is knocked to the floor and arrested for carrying perfume, you have to ask yourself, how far is too far?" Robin turns to Paige now — and so do I ... and my sister is fast asleep.

Robin laughs. "Paige? Paige Forrester?"

I elbow Paige and her head snaps to attention. "Wh — what?"

"I must say this is a first." Robin chuckles. "I don't think I ever had a guest fall asleep on me before. I guess I need to watch out for that boredom factor."

Paige literally looks like a deer in the headlights now. And I know I need to jump in. "My sister is still recovering from yesterday's incident," I say quickly. "It was very traumatic. Then, as a result of our interrogation, we missed our flight and our luggage was lost. And Paige was so stressed that she couldn't sleep well last night and—"

"And this is Erin Forrester," Robin says warmly, "Paige Forrester's sister and costar of their new reality show *On the Runway*. Erin, how about if you tell us what happened yesterday."

So, thankful for Robin's diversion away from Sleeping Beauty, I go into a fairly detailed description of the airport security incident, about the less-than-three-ounce rule and how the Prada was barely over that. "And I couldn't believe how it went down," I continue. "Out of nowhere these two burly guys jumped Paige from behind. I mean, they actually tackled her and knocked her to the ground. See that bruise on her cheek—it's where her face hit the floor. They could've broken something. Even her neck. Or her back when this one guy pinned her down with his knee like she was going to hurt someone."

"They actually pinned her to the ground?"

"Yes. I'm sure it's all on their surveillance cams. And she was screaming in pain and they wouldn't even stop holding her down." Then I hold up my wrists, which still have the red marks from the handcuffs, and explain about that.

"All this for spritzing perfume?" Robin looks stunned.

"Unbelievably, yes. And Paige even admitted that she shouldn't have sprayed it. But for them to assume it was something toxic seemed ridiculous, considering she'd sprayed it on herself. Who would spray themselves with hazardous materials?"

"It was just Prada," Paige says in a slightly hopeless way. "Prada Infusion d'Iris ..."

"So, Paige?" Robin's eyes twinkle. "You awake now?"

"Yes. Sorry about that. But it really was a horrible experience." And then Paige goes on to tell—in even more detail this time—about the strip search and how humiliating and frightening it was. "I asked them several times why I couldn't have my attorney present, but they wouldn't even listen."

"It sounds as if your civil rights went straight out the window once you were taken into custody."

"Exactly." Paige nods eagerly. "I actually felt like I was a criminal in some hostile country. At one point, I almost expected them to lock me up in a dark, damp dungeon with only bread and water."

"And no Prada," Robin teases.

Paige laughs. "No ... definitely, no Prada. In fact, they confiscated my perfume."

Robin goes on to tell that their producer tried to get some

comments from the security guards on their responsibility for the incident, but they were unwilling to be interviewed.

"I'm not surprised." Paige nods.

And then Robin reads a quote from TSA that basically says what I was told about how airport security is to keep everyone safe ... yada-yada. "However," Robin continues, "we did discover several cases which are pending in court. How about you, Paige. Will your case wind up in court?"

Paige pauses to consider this. "I'm not sure. I think I would accept a sincere apology from the female security guard who overreacted, along with the news that the thugs who tackled me have been placed on probation. I just don't like to think that other young women—or anyone—would suffer like I did. It was inhumane."

Robin winds down our interview, takes the cue that it's time for Sam to go to weather, then thanks us and shakes our hands. "I didn't realize it was so traumatic," she tells us as the sound guy removes our mics. "You girls probably need to go back to your hotel and get some rest."

I nod. "I didn't sleep at all last night."

And just like that, we're done. Fran meets up with us outside of the greenroom and then we quietly ride the town car back to our hotel. Thankfully the traffic has let up, and this trip only takes ten minutes. We go directly back to our room, where I'm determined to go straight to bed and only bed. And I'm halfway there when I hear a blood-curdling scream coming from the bathroom. My heart pounds like a sledge hammer as I rush to our bathroom expecting to see my sister being held by a crazed assassin with a knife to her throat, but instead she is simply looking at the mirror.

"*What is it?*" I demand, clutching my chest and wondering

if I might be experiencing cardiac arrest. Maybe that's what sleep deprivation does to a person.

"Look at me!" she shrieks.

"*What?*"

"You let me go on national TV looking like *this*?"

Fran has joined us, and she is standing behind me and giggling.

"We tried to help you," I attempt.

"You tried?" She turns and stares at us. "What—were you blindfolded or something?"

"Hey, you looked even worse before we cleaned you up," Fran tells her.

"You're my sister, Erin, you're supposed to help me." She narrows her eyes at me. "Why did you let me out of the hotel room like this?"

Now I'm upset. I mean, I did *everything* I could to help her and this is the thanks I get. "Yeah, maybe we should've just locked you up," I say. "And thrown away the key."

Paige turns and looks at herself again. "This is truly frightening."

"It just proves that no one, not even Paige Forrester, should attempt to apply cosmetics while under the influence," Fran teases.

"I cannot believe the whole world saw me like this." Now she sounds like she's about to cry again and, seriously, I don't think I can take it. I don't even care.

"You did great on the interview," Fran assures her.

"Yeah, once you woke up," I add. Okay, unnecessary, but so was her screaming and accusations.

"And I'm sure anyone watching felt sorry for you. The sympathy factor was running high."

"Right—they are sorry for my hair and my makeup." Paige is holding out her stringy-looking hair. "I want to go somewhere to die!"

"Go to bed," Fran says firmly. "We all just need to chill for a few hours. Then we'll regroup and figure this thing out."

"I'm ruined," Paige moans.

"I'm exhausted," I say as I head back to my bed. I'm irked at my sister's prima donna attitude. And I can't believe I have thirteen more days to put up with her in New York. For this I should get battle pay!

# Chapter
## 10

*We all sleep for a couple of hours until we wake* to the sound of someone at the door. It seems our lost luggage has finally found its way to our hotel. The bellboy rolls in a brass cart loaded with a small mountain of pink luggage, as well as a few other bags, and Paige breaks into her happy dance. I can't help but smile as I see my sister's eyes light up like Christmas as she embraces her cosmetic bag. But at least she's in a better mood. In fact we all are, and it doesn't hurt that she's getting tweets and texts and emails and all kinds of encouragement from sympathetic fans.

"How about we clean up and go out for a late lunch," Fran suggests. "And maybe do some shopping or see some sights."

"Yes!" exclaims Paige. "I want to see Saks Fifth Avenue, Lord and Taylor, Bergdorf Goodman, Tiffany's—"

"And I'd like to see the Museum of Modern Art," I add.

"All very doable," Fran assures us. "And tonight I have a surprise for you."

"What kind of a surprise?" I ask.

"A surprise-surprise." Fran has a mischievous grin.

Now this has me worried. What if she or Helen have arranged for us to do something with publicity? What if we'll be on camera again? I feel like I need some space from the limelight, if only for a day.

"Don't frown like that, Erin. It'll be fun," she assures me.

"Yeah," calls Paige as she totes her bags off to the bathroom where I'm guessing she'll spend at least an hour repairing her face and hair. "This is New York City—we're supposed to have some fun."

"Hey, I'm totally down with fun," I tell them. "I just want to make sure it's not work-related fun, you know?"

Fran laughs then lowers her voice. "Okay, I get you. Don't tell Paige, but I happen to have three really good tickets to *Wicked.*"

"You're kidding!" I nod eagerly. "*That* sounds like fun."

Not surprisingly I'm dressed and ready to roll, but Paige is just emerging from the shower. And while I understand her need for a second shower with the right shampoos and things, I'm antsy to get out there and see some of the city.

"Why don't you grab a taxi and head on over to MoMA," Fran tells me when she finds me pacing in the living room.

"Momma?"

"M-o-M-A—Museum of Modern Art."

"Oh, right."

"It's not too far from the shopping district, and we can meet up for lunch."

"You don't mind?"

"No. I'll give you a call when I figure out where and when we can meet. You might want to grab a quick street snack in the meantime though."

So just like that I am *free*. With my digital camera in

my backpack, I head down the elevator and the next thing I know I'm cruising through midtown Manhattan in the back of a yellow cab. And soon I'm looking up at the Museum of Modern Art and munching on a giant pretzel. Life is good. I start off with the photography section, trying to take it all in and feeling slightly overwhelmed ... and inspired. Then I go up to look at paintings and sculptures. I'm amazed and impressed with the selection of artists—there's Cézanne and Gauguin and Picasso and so many more that it too is almost overwhelming. But it's Van Gogh's *Starry Night* painting that captivates me and I stare at it for quite some time.

I'm just checking out the lineup of films and trailers offered at the museum when my phone rings and it's time to meet Fran and Paige for a very late lunch. Fran tells me the name of the restaurant and I reluctantly leave MoMA with a promise to myself to come back here during my next "day off." I really want to see the Mike Nichols exhibition if I get the chance.

"So what do you think of New York so far?" Fran asks after I join them in a small Italian restaurant near the shopping district.

"Very cool," I tell her as I look over the menu. "I think I could spend several days at MoMA alone without getting even slightly bored."

Paige holds up a Bergdorf Goodman bag and smirks. "And Fran practically dragged me away from the Bergdorf Goodman cosmetics counter."

"Yes, after being without her makeup for twenty-four hours, you'd think the girl had died and gone to heaven."

"Hey." Paige shakes a finger at Fran. "Ask anyone in fashion about how they'd feel being forced onto national TV without their own personal makeup and I'm sure they'd feel the same."

"Not to mention that you were drugged up," I add.

"And recovering from a security mugging." Fran nods. "Okay, we'll cut you some slack this time, Paige."

"Thank you."

Because we're all starving and because this is an Italian restaurant, we have no problem figuring out what to eat. I go for their lasagna, Paige tries the chicken parmesan, and Fran goes all out with a small pizza.

"Tomorrow I go on a diet," Paige announces after we're done.

"Hey, this was our first real meal in two days," I tell her.

"And we'll have to call it an early dinner too," Fran points out.

"Does Paige know where we're going tonight?" I ask.

"You mean you know?" Paige puts on a pouty face.

"Okay, fine," Fran tells her. "I've got tickets to *Wicked*!"

"Sweet!" Paige is all smiles now. "I've been dying to see that. I heard they were coming to LA, but this is way better."

I'm not sure if it's the lasagna or the lack of sleep last night or just plain jet lag, but I'm seriously sleepy now. "I don't know about you guys," I tell them. "But I want to be awake for the musical so maybe I'll head back to the hotel for a nap."

"Not me," Paige announces. "I plan to shop for at least another hour or two."

So, once again, we part ways. As I hop in a cab to return to the hotel, I'm thinking how great it is to have this unexpected little break today. It's like a Paige break. As much as I love my sister, I needed it. Back at the hotel, it's fun having the whole place to myself. I try to imagine what it would be like if

*I* was the Prima Donna Princess instead of Paige. How would it feel to have everyone catering to me, ironing my clothes, ordering me strawberries, making me a bath? But then I'm sure I'd just feel silly. Really, I'd rather do it for myself. And so I make my own cup of green tea and I draw my own steaming bubble bath ... and finally I snag the cashmere blanket and get into the neatly made bed (compliments of housekeeping) to settle down for a nice relaxing nap.

By the time I wake up it's after six and Paige is coming into the room with a bunch of shopping bags, going on and on about how great the shopping in New York is and how it beats LA. And she's trying on a new pair of lime green shoes and squirting herself with perfume.

"Prada Infusion d'Iris ... sent here by Prada." She sighs dreamily. "Along with a bunch of other Prada goodies too. Can you believe it, Erin? Prada knows my name."

"Who exactly is Prada anyway?" I sit up in bed and watch her. "I mean, I know that Michael Kors is Michael Kors—at least I think he is."

"Kors was actually born Karl Anderson Jr.," Paige informs me.

"But he's a real person, right?"

She's removing something from a large bag. "Yes, a real person." She holds up a pale green dress with a bold black stripe running diagonally through it and smiles.

"And Ralph Lauren is really Ralph Lauren and Liz Claiborne was really Liz Claiborne and Tommy Hilfiger is—"

"Erin?" Paige pulls her eyes away from the striking dress and stares at me like I'm nuts. "What exactly *is* your point?"

"Who is Prada?"

"Oh." She laughs. "Well, Prada is the family name and the

name of the company. It was just leather back when it was started by Fratelli and Mario Prada, back in Milan, like about one hundred years ago."

"Seriously?"

She nods then turns to look at herself in the mirror as she holds up the dress like she's trying to see how it goes with the shoes—and I have to admit it actually looks really good. "And later on Mario's daughter-in-law ... or maybe it was his granddaughter—I can't remember exactly—but Miuccia Prada came on board, like in the seventies, I think. Remember I told you about Miu Miu?"

I just nod.

"Well, Miu Miu is her line, which came later. So anyway, in the seventies, Miuccia began to modernize the House of Prada by producing things beyond luggage. She came out with the famous Prada handbag and then went on to belts and a pretty sleek line of clothes that was totally revolutionary to fashion in the eighties and then, of course, their shoes." She holds out a foot. "They are rather famous for their shoes."

"So is *Miuccia* Prada the Prada we're talking about when we're talking about Prada?"

Paige gives me a tolerant smile as she carefully removes the pale green dress from the padded hanger. "Yes, something like that ... you're learning."

"And so Miuccia sent you the perfume?"

She laughs "Well, not personally. But someone in the House of Prada did. And that's enough for me."

As she slips on the dress, I decide maybe it's time to get out of bed and think about getting dressed myself.

"How do I look?" she asks as she turns around to show me her outfit.

"Fantastic," I tell her. "That color is really good on you."

"Guess which designer?"

I go for the obvious. "Prada?"

"Close." She chuckles. "*Miu Miu.*" And now she's strutting back and forth between our bedroom and bathroom like she's in a fashion show.

"Pretty funny," I tell her. "You looked like something the cat dragged in this morning and tonight you look like you could do the Prada *cat*walk."

She chuckles. "Well, thank you ... I guess." Her hair flips as she does a quick turn then stops suddenly, turning to me as if an idea has just occurred to her. "You know, Erin, Prada is one of the few designers who actually features new models at Fashion Week ..." Her forehead creases as if she's in deep thought, but then she shakes her head. "But, no, even if they asked, I think I'd have to decline. I need to keep my role in fashion clear. I am Paige Forrester, fashion expert for *On the Runway*. Not a model."

"Seriously?" I study her closely. "Are you saying that if Miuccia Prada herself asked you to be in her big show next week, you would simply tell her to forget it?"

She shrugs. "Oh, I don't know about that. But let's just say that's *not* going to happen." Now she frowns at me. "Good grief, Erin, aren't you going to get ready for the theater? We should be leaving in about thirty minutes."

"I'm up already," I tell her. "And, don't worry, you know it never takes me as long as you."

"Yes, and we won't go into that right now since I still need to do my makeup and hair."

I want to point out that her hair and makeup already look perfect, but I realize I might as well talk to the wall. Instead I go to my bag, which I haven't fully unpacked yet, and I begin pulling things out. I soon have a pile of clothes on the floor, but I quickly discover that I don't have anything nearly as swanky as Paige's outfit.

Now it's not that I want to look like her, but I realize I might've blown it by not packing something more theater-friendly. And, although I know we have a bunch of great designer clothes—most of which I ironed last night—I also know they're supposed to be for when we're doing the show or publicity. Both Helen and Fran made that perfectly clear before we left LA. So I can't go there. I finally decide on my black turtleneck sweater, denim skirt, leather jacket, and boots. I systematically lay them out on the bed and begin to dress.

"What are you doing?" Paige demands.

I've just pulled my sweater over my head and peer out the top hole of the turtleneck. "Huh?"

*"What on earth are you putting on?"*

"My clothes."

"But we're going to *the theater*, Erin. This is *New York*. We might even be *seen* tonight."

I kind of laugh. "Yeah, unless we suddenly become invisible."

She goes over and picks up my denim skirt, holding it like it's a soured dishrag that's been in the sink too long. "You are *so* not wearing this, Erin Forrester. Seriously. What's wrong with you?"

"I didn't pack anything very dressy," I admit.

She frowns and stomps off to the living room, where I can hear her complaining to Fran. "Erin has totally lost it. I cannot believe she's this hopelessly fashion-challenged." Now I go out there, in just my turtleneck and underwear, and stand behind her and listen as she goes on about how pathetic I am. "My very own sister and she has absolutely no sense of style—none whatsoever. And this is Manhattan and next week is Fashion Week and we're supposed to be the stars of *On the Runway* and she's putting on an outfit that totally—"

"Calm down," Fran holds up her hands to stop her then looks at me curiously. "That what you're wearing tonight, Erin?"

I look down at my bare legs. "Well, no ... I planned to put on a skirt."

To my surprise they both laugh at this. And I'm slightly relieved to have lightened the moment—albeit at my expense.

"I didn't really pack anything formal," I explain, apologizing.

"But this is Manhattan and you were supposed—"

"Paige," Fran interrupts. "Chill out. And go finish your makeup or whatever you were doing. I'll handle this."

Paige groans and turns around, stomping back to the bathroom.

"I'm sorry," I tell Fran. "I just packed things for what I figured I'd want to do during my spare time, like see the Statue of Liberty or MoMA or take in a film. No big deal, you know."

"Yes. I understand, but Paige is making a good point too. And since she's right—you girls could be seen tonight, you could even be photographed—we need to think of this as a publicity appearance and you need to look hot."

"Fine." I shrug. "I have no problem with that ... if it's even possible."

Fran laughs then goes to the closet where she begins to peruse through the studio clothes and finally pulls out a charcoal gray dress. "It doesn't look like much without the accessories," she says as she hands it to me. "It's Marc Jacobs. Go ahead and put it on while I round up the belt and shoes."

I slip the dress on and look at it in the mirror. It's not terribly special looking, but I have to admit it looks much better than what I was about to wear. Very classic lines and elegant.

"Here you go," Fran tells me as she hands me a shiny yellow belt and a box that has a pair of yellow and black pumps inside.

I put them on and then look at myself again. "Not bad," I tell her.

"I'd say it's pretty good." Fran puts a long silver necklace around my neck, then steps back and smiles.

Now Paige emerges from the bathroom and looks me up and down. "*Tres chic*," she says with an approving nod.

"So, fashion emergency averted?" I ask. "I'm allowed to go out with you tonight?"

"With a little makeup," Paige says as she pushes me toward the bathroom.

"I'm going to look like the ugly ducking," Fran calls after us.

And although Fran looks nice enough in her little black dress and pumps, as the three of us wait to go into the theater on 51st Street I have to admit that Paige and I look great. And we do catch people's eyes. I can tell they're looking at us like they're trying to figure out who we are. And, although it's hard to admit, I suppose it's actually kind of fun.

# Chapter 11

"*Bad news,*" *Fran tells us Saturday morn-*ing as we're having breakfast in our room. She's studying her BlackBerry with a dark frown. "Our camera crew never made it into New York last night. They're stuck in Chicago—unexpected blizzard."

"Does that mean we cancel on the Dylan Marceau visit today?" Paige asks with a worried brow.

"No way," Fran tells her. "We worked really hard to set that one up and if we don't show we might never get the chance again. Dylan is getting more and more in demand and we don't want to offend him."

"I could film the visit with my camera," I say. "The quality won't be as high as the crew's cameras, but at least we'll have some footage."

"And at least we won't blow off the appointment and offend the Dylan Marceau people," Fran adds.

"And possibly get ourselves uninvited to his show next week." Paige refills her coffee cup. "That would be really sad."

"You really think you can handle this on your own?" Fran asks me.

"I'll do my best." I try not to look too happy because I know I should be as bummed as they are about losing our camera crew today. But the truth is I'm totally excited to think I'm not just "playing" Camera Girl today, but actually doing it. And that means two things: One, I do not need to worry about being filmed and two, with the crew stuck in Chicago I have a chance to get the best shots. Or so I hope.

"I'll let JJ know where we'll be just in case they catch a flight and make it here in time to come over and help us out." Fran goes into the kitchen to make the call and we hear snippets of the conversation. "Still snowing? Well, there's nothing you can do about that." Fran sighs loudly. "Erin's going to try to get some footage. Sure, I'll tell her. You kids just take care and get here as soon as you can." Then she says good-bye. "Sounds pretty bad," she tells us. "They spent the night in the airport and it doesn't look like anything will be flying out for at least two more hours."

I know I shouldn't feel as pleased as I do. And to make up for this, I silently pray for the crew's welfare and safety.

"And JJ said to tell you that you'll do fine, Erin. He said just relax and film your subjects like you're just watching them."

"Just *watching* them?"

"Those were his words."

I nod. "Okay, that kind of makes sense." I also want to say that his advice sounds like an oversimplification to me, but then again, JJ's the expert. Not me. Hopefully this will be a good learning experience.

We arrive at the Dylan Marceau studio a little before ten.

I'm not really sure who this designer is, but I know that Paige is totally excited to meet him and Fran seemed really pleased that we lined him up for an interview. So I'm thinking this guy must be one of the "top designers" and therefore I brace myself for someone who's a little too full of himself.

"I'm Autumn," a small brunette tells us after the receptionist announces our arrival. "Dylan's creative director."

"Hi, Autumn, I'm Paige Forrester," Paige says as she hands her business card to the woman. "Unfortunately, our camera crew is stuck in Chicago due to bad weather." She nods toward me and makes a quick introduction. "But Erin is an experienced camera operator and I'm sure we won't be disappointed."

"Great," Autumn says. "Sounds like we're ready to rock and roll. And I'm actually relieved that you don't have a huge crew with you. Hopefully that will streamline the tour and speed things up a bit, because as you know, we're crunching on some serious deadlines here."

"And we want to be totally respectful of your time."

As they're talking I turn on my camera, plug in the mic, and adjust the lens. And, just like that, we're off and running. Autumn proceeds to give us what has become the typical tour of a design studio. And, really, this place isn't much different than the ones in LA. However, there does seem to be some positive energy here. The designers are really into their work, but maybe that's just because Fashion Week is coming fast. I do notice that the spaces here seem smaller than some of the LA studios, but I suspect that's because Manhattan real estate is scarcer than it is at home. The largest room is where the actual garment construction happens, and that space is a whirl of activity and actually pretty fun to catch on camera. Paige doesn't even go in there, and I try to get as much footage of the cutters and sewers as I can before Autumn whisks us on our way.

There's also a fitting room, where we get a glimpse of models and mannequins with garments in various stages of construction, and I catch what I hope might be some interesting footage. And there's the usual conference room, offices, a shipping room, and a few other less-interesting spaces, as well as a room which is posted "Authorized Personnel Only." Autumn winks into the lens of the camera as she points to the sign. "And that, as you can guess, is top secret until next week."

We finally end up in what Autumn describes as the "nerve center" for the whole operation. The lower portions of the walls contain sleek built-in cabinets with large drawers and open shelves that hold sketchbooks, photograph albums, and magazines. The upper portions of two walls are like giant drawing boards and have some random sketches of clothing scribbled here and there—almost like graffiti. Another wall is a colorful collage of fabric swatches and trims and things. The fourth wall has photos of finished garments and shots from various fashion shows. And there's an oversized desk in the center and several molded plastic chairs in varying colors around it. The total effect is creatively pleasing and it's fun to get on camera.

"This is where Dylan gets his brainstorms," Autumn explains. "In other words: Design Central." She opens one of the sketchbooks and I focus my shot on it as she flips through the pages. "Naturally, this is a book from a previous season." She chuckles and I move the camera to her face. "As you know, some parts of this business must remain under wraps until the time is right." She glances at her watch. "Speaking of time, I apologize for Dylan. He seems to be running late."

"So, tell me, Autumn." Paige just keeps it going. "What got you into this kind of work? And can you tell us about what a creative director does?"

"Sure. I actually got my degree in design and I really wanted to be a designer," Autumn admits. "And maybe someday I will. But I was lucky to join Dylan's team a few years ago when he was just starting up. I could tell he was brilliant and far more ready for this than I was. So I signed on as an assistant and worked my way up to this position. Let's see ... a creative director actually oversees a lot of things, including all forms of publicity and marketing—from arranging photo shoots to running print ads to planning our actual fashion shows and—"

"Hello, ladies." I fan my camera around to catch a sandy-haired guy coming into the room. "Sorry to be late."

"And this is Dylan Marceau," Autumn announces.

"I want to accommodate your show," he says, "but I can only give you about fifteen minutes."

Now Dylan, who actually seems quite young, takes Autumn's chair and Paige wastes no time as she jumps in with her regular questions. But Dylan's responses are much friendlier than I expected. This guy isn't snooty at all. In fact, it could be my imagination, but I think he likes my sister. Their conversation gets snappy and witty and pretty lively.

And that's when I realize I'm over my head because we really need two cameras to properly catch a conversation like this. Still I back up, open up the lens, and just do my best to keep up. And like JJ said, I just pretend I'm watching them chat and after awhile, it's like I get into this rhythm and I'm hopeful that maybe, just maybe, it will work.

"Sorry to cut this short," Dylan finally tells Paige. Although I think it's been longer than his originally promised fifteen minutes—in fact, according to my camcorder it's been more than fifty-four minutes. "But I'm totally buried today. I decided to do some last-minute changes and, well, I'm sure you can imagine what it's like." He reaches out to shake Paige's hand. "But I did enjoy our time together."

"So did I," Paige assures him. "And I totally appreciate you taking time out of your busy day. I didn't mention it earlier because I didn't want to sound too schmoozy, but I've been a fan of yours for a while and it was an incredible honor to actually meet you."

"Maybe when Fashion Week is over we can do this again," he tells her. "With our without your camera crew."

Paige's eyes light up. "Absolutely!"

"And if you'd like to talk to anyone else," he says as he pauses by the door, "maybe Autumn can help. There are a few models just hanging around, killing time between fittings. You might be able to catch one of them for a few words about what that particular angle of fashion is like."

"That'd be great. Thanks again!" He exits and Paige turns back to Autumn. "Do you think we could round up a model or two?"

"Certainly," Autumn tells her. "Let me call Jill in fitting to see if there's someone she can send our way."

I use this opportunity to check my camera's batteries and memory card and to make sure I'm ready to keep shooting if we get the chance. And the next thing I know a tall, beautiful young woman with dark curly hair and skin the color of a creamy latte comes in. "Hi, I'm Taylor Mitchell," she says. "Jill asked me to stop by."

"*Taylor Mitchell.*" Paige stands and extends her hand. "It's such an honor to meet you. I am such a fan."

Taylor laughs and it's a hearty, genuine-sounding laugh. "Seriously?" she asks. "How do you even know who I am?"

"Oh, you'd be surprised at what I know about fashion."

I'd like to ditto that, but I'm too busy trying to get some good footage of Taylor. She is really stunning and yet she seems real too — full of life.

"For starters, I know that you're about the same age as I am," Paige continues. "And that you started modeling professionally under the supervision of Katherine Carter, former model and ex-editor-in-chief of *Couture* magazine."

"Wow, you really do your homework." Taylor looks impressed.

"And I know that you're Dylan Marceau's favorite model, but I thought I heard you were a free agent, so to speak. Aren't you modeling for a number of designers now?"

"Yes, but I still try to give Dylan some of my time too. He's a great guy — and a brilliant designer."

"I couldn't agree more. I predict Dylan will be leading the way in design before long — maybe even next season. But, Taylor, it seems you've actually had something to do with Dylan's recent success."

"Oh, I don't know about that." Taylor frowns slightly now, like she's a little confused. "I'm sorry ... but did you say who you were exactly?"

I can't help but laugh. Paige actually *did* forget to introduce herself. This is a first for my smooth sister!

"I'm sorry," Paige quickly recovers. "I'm Paige Forrester

from *On the Runway*, and the girl behind the camera is my sister, Erin. Our camera crew got stuck in a Midwest blizzard."

Taylor laughs. "Oh, good. I thought maybe you were from a local high school, trying to get something for your school's website. Not that I wouldn't talk to them, but this is a pretty busy time for everyone."

Paige just smiles. "Yes, we're usually a bit more professional than this, but we didn't want to miss the chance to meet Dylan."

"So you're the girls who are staying at our house next week?" Taylor continues with interest.

"Yes, if that's okay. Apparently our boss, Helen Hudson, and your mom are friends."

"Absolutely. It'll be fun. Eliza is acting like we're having a slumber party."

"Eliza?"

"My roommate."

"And she's a model too, right?"

Taylor nods, but I suspect by the look in her eyes that she's not too sure about this roommate. Or maybe she's just not sure the girl is model material. I'm thinking maybe spending a night at their place might provide some interesting stories after all.

Paige continues to ask Taylor fashion and modeling questions and it seems like the two of them are really hitting it off. In fact, before we're done, it's as if the table has been turned and suddenly Taylor is interviewing Paige. She's curious as to how Paige got her start in TV and what kind of training she's had. Fortunately, Paige just goes with the flow. And I'm glad because I think it's going to make for some good material for our show.

"Well, this has been fun," Taylor finally says, "but I really need to get over to the Ralph Lauren studio now. They're doing some fittings today too."

"I wish we could go with you," Paige says longingly. "We tried to set up an interview over there, but they were just too busy."

"I'm not surprised." Taylor smiles. "But hopefully you can make it to his show. It's going to be good."

"We're working on it," Fran says from where she's sitting in a corner reading a magazine, and we all look her way. "But so far it sounds like they're full."

"Maybe I could help," Taylor offers. "Not that I have some magic touch, but I *am* friends with the guy in charge of seating." She chuckles as she reaches for her bag. "A few of my friends are nagging me for tickets."

"Oh, if you could help us out, we'd really appreciate it." Paige hands Taylor her business card.

"In fact ..." Taylor gets a thoughtful look across her brow. "Maybe we could exchange favors."

"What do you have in mind?"

"If I can get you into the Ralph Lauren show ... how about if you interview a designer friend of mine in return, to get her some exposure?"

"Of course," Paige agrees. "We'd love to interview your friend."

"Great!" Taylor grins. "I'll get back to you on the Ralph Lauren tickets." Then she tells us all good-bye and leaves.

"Wow." Paige sits down and sighs. "That was awesome. This has been such a productive day." She suddenly looks at me with concern. "You did get all that, didn't you, Erin?"

"I did the best I could. I suppose it'll be up to the editors to decide whether it makes it on the show or not."

And as we pack up to go, I shoot up a quick prayer—okay, so maybe it's a backward sort of prayer. I wonder if it's possible to pray in reverse. Anyway, I ask God to bless the filming that just took place and to hopefully make it usable for our show.

# Chapter

## 12

"Did it seem like Dylan was into me?" Paige asks later that evening when we're all just crashing in our pajamas in the hotel suite.

"I think he's just friendly like that," Fran says as she flips through the channels on the TV.

Paige looks unconvinced. "I don't know ... usually I have pretty good instincts about guys. It seemed like he was into me."

"It kind of did to me too," I admit.

Just then her phone rings and I can tell by the tone of Paige's voice that it's Benjamin on the other end. She starts out very cool and formal and then suddenly she's telling him about Dylan and how great the interview went and how she thinks Dylan is "into her."

Fran and I exchange glances, but Paige seems totally oblivious to the way she sounds as she rambles on and on about Dylan and his studio, but eventually she switches over to talking about the interview with Taylor Mitchell. "And she seems like she's looking forward to having us stay in their apartment." She pauses to listen and probably catch her breath. "Well, yeah, she's hot. Maybe even better-looking in person than in print. I don't know, Benjamin. I mean it's not like we're BFFs or anything." She pauses. "Fine." Her voice is crisp now. "I'll ask her." And then the conversation winds down and Paige snaps her phone closed.

"Can you believe that?" she says to us.

"What?" I ask as I flip through the photography magazine I've been studying.

"Benjamin wants me to arrange for him to meet Taylor Mitchell."

I can't help but laugh.

"What's so funny?"

"Obviously, you couldn't hear yourself talking to him." I look over to Fran, but she's engrossed in a new reality TV show.

"What do you mean?" Paige demands.

"You were going on and on about Dylan, saying how you thought he was into you and it sounded more like you were crushing on Dylan. I'm sure Benjamin was just jealous."

Now Paige smiles ... but it's a catty smile. "You think?"

"Oh, I don't know." I stand and stretch. "Maybe Benjamin really does want to meet Taylor. I mean, the girl is stunning."

Now Paige frowns and I think my work here is done. "Good night," I say as I head off to bed.

The next day, Sunday, is officially our day off. We all sleep in until almost noon and then agree to do as we like with the remainder of the day and to reconvene for dinner in the hotel restaurant at six. Fran wants to make it an early evening so we can be fresh in the morning. "The camera crew will meet us at Marc Jacobs at nine o'clock sharp, and I want the whole thing to go as smoothly as yesterday—only with the full crew. This is a big opportunity and there's no room for error."

Paige tries to talk me into going shopping with her, but I beg out. "I already bought a ticket online for the MoMA," I explain. "I'm going to take in the film exhibits and watch some trailers and things. But you're welcome to come with me. It's really an amazing—"

"No thanks."

"I have an idea," Fran tells Paige. "Why don't we go to the fashion museum at FIT?"

Paige seems interested and I take this as my cue to make a getaway. I feel a little bit guilty bailing on my sister like that, but I can only handle so much of her fashion obsession. Although I must admit the fashion museum might be interesting ... on another day.

After a couple of hours of film indulgence, I take a break and get a soda at the café, taking a moment to turn on my phone. As I listen to a voicemail from Mom, returning my call to her this morning with a sweet message about how she and Jon are driving to Balboa today but that she'd rather be with her two girls, I feel oddly homesick. The next message is from Blake, just checking in to see how it's going. We talked yesterday, but I decide to give him a call just the same.

"Hey," he says cheerfully. "I was just thinking about you."

"Really?"

"Yeah. I just got out of church and I'm sitting in my car, still in the parking lot, and wondering what I'm going to do with myself for the day. I was wishing you were here so we could hang out together. It's a gorgeous day."

"Lucky you," I tell him. "It's cold and cloudy in New York."

"I'd gladly put up with rain, sleet, and snow just to be there with you."

"Kind of like a mailman, eh?"

He chuckles. "Yes, I'm that faithful sort. You can count on me."

"Did you see Mollie at church?" I'm not even sure why I ask this; I guess I'm just curious.

"No. In fact, she and Tony weren't at the fellowship last night either."

"Oh."

"So, where are you right now?" he asks.

I tell him about MoMA and he acts like he's totally jealous. Then I tell him about how Paige thinks Dylan Marceau is into her and how Benjamin wants to meet Taylor Mitchell. We talk and laugh for about half an hour and by the time we hang up, I don't feel homesick anymore. I even decide to give Mollie a call and am slightly taken aback when she answers.

"Hey, Mollie," I say cheerfully.

"Erin?" She sounds almost happy, like she's glad I called — and that surprises me.

"Yeah. How are you? I was thinking about you and decided to see what's up."

"Not much. I kind of slept in this morning … missed church. What's up?"

"Well, it's been awhile since we talked."

"Yeah … Where are you?"

So I tell her about MoMA and the cool film exhibits I've been enjoying.

*"You're in New York?"*

"Remember, I told you awhile back that we were doing Fashion Week in early February."

"I guess. But the date seemed so far out there … and now New York seems far away …" Her voice trails off.

So, in an attempt to fill the space, I tell her about the Dylan Marceau interview and how I was the whole camera crew, but instead of making the kinds of comments or questions you expect in a normal conversation, Mollie is silent and it makes me almost wonder if we're disconnected. "Are you still there?"

"Yeah ... I guess so."

"You guess so?" Okay, that's a weird response. And it kind of hurts my feelings. Like, am I so boring that she's fallen asleep on me? Or maybe she has something more important to do? Perhaps she's actually watching TV and only pretending to listen to me.

"I'm feeling a little under the weather," she says.

"Sorry to hear that. The flu?"

"Yeah, probably."

"Yuck."

"Yeah."

"Well, I should let you go, Mollie."

"Yeah ... I guess."

Now her voice sounds so sad that I almost want to demand to know what's going on. But then I think if she's got the flu, that's probably depressing enough. "Well, you take care. Drink lots of green tea and get some rest."

"I will." She sighs loudly. "And you take care in New York. Have fun."

"Thanks." Then we hang up and I just shake my head. What is wrong with Mollie? Well, other than the flu. Or maybe nothing's wrong. Maybe I'm just blowing things out of proportion.

Our hair and makeup stylists show up at the hotel on Monday morning and you'd think Paige had died and gone to beauty heaven. Two hours later, when we arrive at Marc Jacobs, our camera crew is in place and ready to go. It suddenly feels like we're professionals again.

A Marc Jacobs publicity person named Millie meets us and acts as our guide as she gives us what turns out to be a pretty quick tour. But at least Paige gets a chance to meet Marc Jacobs, even if it's only briefly. And he promises to spend more time with her some other day.

"When things aren't so hectic," he calls out as he ducks into a doorway marked "private." Finally it seems our tour has come to an end and Millie takes us to a showroom where a number of Marc Jacobs' finest designs are on display. Nothing for the upcoming season, of course, but the outfits are impressive and I think even I could become a Marc Jacobs fan. His style is clean and understated and classic. I don't know a lot about fashion, but I know that. And I know that it's a look I can appreciate.

"Marc Jacobs is definitely one of a kind," Paige is saying into the cameras in an effort to stretch this thing out. "He certainly doesn't cater to the whims of the crowd—and yet the crowd seems to follow him. And Mr. Jacobs has surprised us more than once in his choices of models. I remember when he used Dakota Fanning a few years back, when she was still a child. All his women's clothes were sized down for her, even the shoes. It was clever and eye-catching. And then there was the scarf scandal." She glances over at Millie now, and it's clear that Millie doesn't appreciate whatever the "scarf scandal" might be. But I know *I'm* curious.

"However, I happen to believe it was simply a mistake," Paige continues with confidence. "I heard that the scarf was actually a flea market find, obviously just something that someone had thrown out. It was only used as a prop in a print ad, and I think it was very self-serving and opportunistic for Olofsson to charge Mr. Jacobs with plagiarism. If anything, Olofsson should have been flattered that Marc chose to use his old scarf." Paige chuckles.

Now Millie is beaming and I can only assume that whatever it is Paige is insinuating has pleased her tremendously.

"This is Paige Forrester," she says with finality, "telling you to always put your best foot forward." She sticks out a tall black boot. "And in this case it would definitely be Marc Jacobs. See you at Fashion Week!"

As the crew shuts down, Millie comes over and shakes Paige's hand. "That was excellent, Paige. And I know Marc will appreciate hearing how fairly you represented the, uh, scarf incident. Thank you." She turns to her assistant. "Make sure that you give them the clothes we set aside." Millie smiles at Paige. "Now if you'll excuse me."

Once the three of us are back in the town car, Fran pats Paige on the back. "You are brilliant, dear. Absolutely brilliant."

"How do you know all this stuff?" I ask as I zip up my backpack. "Was it something you learned at the fashion museum yesterday?"

"The museum was closed," Paige tells me. "But I know how to do my research . . . I never go into an interview without a little something in my back pocket."

"And that probably helped you to leave with a lot of clothes in the trunk as well," Fran says. "I have a feeling if you'd gone the other direction in the scarf story, you'd not only come back empty-handed, but our seats at the Marc Jacobs fashion show would've been mysteriously lost as well."

Tuesday's big interview is at the Kate Spade studio, but once again, the designer is too busy to do an actual sit-down interview. She stops by where we're filming in one of the design rooms to say a quick hello.

"I got my first Kate Spade handbag when I was twelve," Paige tells her. "I begged and begged until my dad finally caved and got it for me. It was pink and camel and I love it to this day, even more so since it reminds me of my father." Paige looks a bit sentimental but then shakes it off.

Kate puts her hand on Paige's arm. "Thank you."

"No," Paige gushes. "*Thank you!* You are both a fabulous designer and a wonderful role model for young women like me and it's an honor to meet you."

Kate nods and smiles. "I hope someday we have time to meet up again. You tell your people to call me and we'll see what we can do."

"Good luck with your show!" Paige calls as Kate leaves.

"I'm not just gushing," Paige says to the cameras. "Kate Spade is a genuine inspiration to any young woman who's into fashion. She was born just a regular Midwestern girl, but blessed with talent and motivation, Kate got a job at *Mademoiselle* and worked her way up in the fashion world. And look where she is now. Some of you may not know that Kate Spade's husband, Andy, is the brother of actor and comedian David Spade. In fact, Kate Spade bags were spotted on an old TV sitcom that David Spade starred in—a show that I used to adore called *Just Shoot Me*." Paige winks at the camera. "I'm guessing that having Nina Van Horn toting a Kate Spade handbag didn't hurt the sales any either."

Paige isn't too excited about Wednesday's interview, and as a result she seems to be dragging her heels this morning. While Fran and I are having coffee downstairs at the hotel (waiting for Paige to come down), Fran tells me about today's assignment. "She's a designer named Paige who used to be a fit model."

"What's a *fit model*?"

"Someone with the kind of body that actually makes clothes look good." Fran laughs. "And I don't mean good as in hanging on a hanger good."

"As in *not* stick thin?"

"That's right. Paige Adams-Geller is a beautiful woman, but not the kind you normally see during Fashion Week. She's five foot seven and has a curvy figure that most women would kill for. Basically, she's not the tall underweight type of girl we're used to watching on the runway. And she's taken a fair amount of heat for it. But some people applaud her courage to be a real woman."

"So she's someone I could relate to?" I venture.

"Absolutely." Fran laughs. "You and me both."

"I think this sounds like a great interview. I mean, think about it, like ninety-eight percent of American women do not look anything like runway models. Or even the ones we see in print ads. And yet that's what gets shoved at us all the time. I, for one, get tired of it."

"I'm with you, Erin. Unfortunately, those are the images that sell fashion. Those are the images that drive our show. Trust me, no one would watch *On the Runway* if we didn't have girls like Taylor Mitchell showing up."

"But what's wrong with having a fashion icon — if that's what Paige is — who is like the rest of us once in a while?"

"Maybe nothing. But don't get me wrong, this woman is *not* like the rest of us," Fran corrects me. "She's gorgeous. She's won pageants and been on TV shows like *Baywatch*. This woman is definitely hot. But I suspect Paige—your sister, Paige—isn't overly impressed with this Paige. And I wasn't either at first. But when I read a little more about her, I thought it could be fun. It was Helen's idea originally: she thought Paige on Paige sounded clever."

So when Paige comes down and we load up into the town car, I try to talk this other Paige up. "I think she sounds very cool," I tell my sister. "And I'm sure our viewers will appreciate seeing someone in fashion who's not into anorexia."

"Actually, Paige Adams-Geller did have anorexia," Paige informs me as she touches up her lip gloss.

"Oh . . ." I'm not sure how to respond to this.

"But maybe that would be a good angle," Paige says slowly. "You could be right, Erin. Maybe that would appeal to viewers who are trying to get a grip on their own appearance. I mean, it's a fact that not everyone can look like a model."

"I can vouch for that," I say.

"And we need to let them know that's okay."

I try not to roll my eyes at the idea of Paige Forrester "kindly" telling her viewers that it's okay that they're not as beautiful as, say, Paige Forrester.

"I think that's how I'll direct this interview," she says as we're getting out of the town car.

And that's just what she does. But to my relief, the other Paige handles it beautifully. She takes no offense at some of Paige's less-than-sensitive comments and questions and, when we're wrapping it up, I step up and shake her hand.

"I really appreciate your honesty," I tell her. "I know that

I get fed up with the idea that everyone needs to be skinny to look good in clothes. And you prove that's wrong. I wish we had more people in the fashion industry who were willing to take your position."

"Thanks, Erin." She looks at me. "And I think I've got a few pairs of jeans that you might like to try out."

"Really?"

She nods to her assistant. "Get her size and her address and see that she's sent a good selection, okay?"

Once we're back in the car, Fran informs me that the cameras were still running while I was talking to Paige Adams-Geller.

"They were?" I frown in disappointment.

"And I'm glad they were. I plan to encourage the editors to include that bit. Our viewers need to hear you saying what you said. They'll relate." Fran's making a note. "Also, we need to put our people in touch with Paige Premium Denim to see about running an ad."

"Oh, great," Paige says with sarcasm. "Now we'll have jean ads on our show."

I make a face at my sister. "Yeah, and that would be worse than, say, tampon ads? Get over yourself, Paige!"

# Chapter 13

*On Thursday morning, we are invited back* to *Good Morning America*, and our interviewer is Diane Sawyer. And this time Paige doesn't make a fool of herself. Instead, she talks with confidence and expertise about our TV show and how we'll be covering Fashion Week. And I just sit there like a prop.

"But what about you, little sister?" Diane directs this question to me. "What's your role in this new show?"

"I'm the camera girl," I say awkwardly. "I sort of just hang out with my camera and pretend to be interested in fashion."

Diane laughs. "Pretend? You mean you're not?"

I'm thinking *oops*. "Uh, yes, I'm a little interested. But Paige is the fashion expert. I'm more into the filming side of things."

"You sound like my husband."

"Oh, yeah!" I say suddenly. "You're married to Mike Nichols, right? I am such a fan of his. He's brilliant!"

She smiles patiently. "I'll pass that along to him."

"You see, I was taking film and TV at UCLA, but I dropped out to do this show, which was a great opportunity ..."

She nods. "Absolutely. Few lessons in the classroom can compare to hands-on field experience." She turns back to Paige now. "Well, I wish you luck with your new show and enjoy Fashion Week and New York."

"Thank you!" Paige beams toward the camera. "I'm enjoying it already."

"And I'm glad to see you recovered from last week's security debacle."

"Yes. That's something I definitely want to put behind me."

And that's it. They go to break, Diane thanks us, our mics are removed, and we are quickly ushered out.

"You *pretend* to be interested in fashion?" Paige hisses at me once we're outside of the studio.

Fran laughs. "Hey, it was honest, Paige. Give the girl a break. Plus, you've got to hand it to Erin ... she recovered quickly."

"It might've been honest, but it sounded totally lame."

"Yeah, whatever." I control myself from saying that Paige sounded just as lame when she told Diane about appearing on *Malibu Beach*, like that was something to brag about.

We return to the hotel for breakfast, followed by a meeting in our room with Fran and the camera crew as we go over the itinerary for the next several days. It seems that some of the designers have now sent press passes for some of the shows that Paige and I already have seats for. So now Fran wants to set it up to film.

"Considering how late we came into this game, we are seeing a fair amount of action," she says as we're wrapping it up. "All those interviews at the design studios really warmed up the waters."

"Talk about mixing your metaphors," JJ—one of the camera guys—teases her.

Fran scowls at him. "Now you and Alistair better figure out a way to decide who gets to go to which show. Flip a coin if necessary."

Paige focuses in on Luis and Shauna, our hair and makeup people. "And you guys will come to our hotel three hours before every fashion show, right?"

"You got it," Luis promises. "Earlier if you like. This place is way nicer than the fleabag motel we're staying at over in New Jersey."

"Three hours before the shows will be plenty of time," Fran assures Paige. "Bryant Park is only a few blocks from here. Even if traffic is a mess, which is likely, we can always walk there in less than twenty minutes."

"What if it's raining?" Paige demands.

"We'll use umbrellas," I suggest.

Paige just glares at me.

"We'll figure something out," Fran promises. "Don't worry."

"And if it's raining," I point out, "we won't be the only ones who are wet."

"Speak for yourself," she tells me. "I do not plan to show up looking like a drowned rat."

"Speaking of bad looks," Luis teases, "nothing can beat that look you had going on at the first *Good Morning America* last week. We watched while we were stuck in O'Hare and enjoyed a good hard laugh."

"Thanks a lot." Paige makes a face. "So compassionate."

"Hey, we needed a laugh," says JJ.

"At least your cheek is back to normal," Shauna tells Paige. "We won't need the extra coverage makeup anymore."

"Quiet, everyone," Fran is telling us. She's on the phone, probably to Helen. "What, can you repeat that?" She waits and listens. "Oh, that's fantastic. Yes, absolutely. I'll call them right away and get it set. Yes, have Sabrina email their numbers. Great." She puts down her phone now and beams at us. "Guess who wants you girls on their shows?"

"Shows?" Paige says hopefully. "As in more than one?"

Fran nods. "Producers from both the *Today* Show and *Live with Regis and Kelly* have contacted Helen about interviewing you during Fashion Week. Isn't that great?"

So we sit back down again, and with everyone there, we go over our schedule, waiting as Fran puts in calls to the producers. It's starting to look like next week is going to be crazy-busy. But that's why we're here.

On Friday morning we first do *The Early Show*, which is even earlier than *GMA* was yesterday. And after that we do the *Today* Show with Kathie Lee and Hoda Kotb, and they turn out to be pretty laid back and a lot of fun. They even invite Paige to critique their outfits and, thankfully, she doesn't say anything too mean or offensive. Mostly it's just humorous. Then, as we're heading back to the hotel in the town car, Paige gets a phone call. "It's Taylor Mitchell," she happily announces as she reads the caller ID.

"Hey, Taylor," she says. "What's up?" She waits and listens. "Really? That is awesome." She pauses again, this time for several minutes. "Yes, I think we can fit it in. Let me check with the powers that be and get back to you ASAP, okay?"

"What's happening?" Fran asks after Paige hangs up.

"Taylor got us tickets to Ralph Lauren *and* an interview with him, if we wait until after his show, which is Saturday night."

"Awesome!" Fran gives Paige a high five.

"What's the hitch?" I ask.

"Taylor wants us to meet her designer friend. She's actually a student at FIT."

"F-I-T?" I question. "As in fit?"

"As in Fashion Institute of Technology," Paige tells me.

"Right." I guess I should've seen that one coming.

"Anyway, her friend's name is Rhiannon and she's interning for a no-name designer, but according to Taylor, Rhiannon has real talent."

"But if she's not really a designer," I begin slowly, "and just an intern attending FIT ... what will you interview her about?"

"I'm not really sure yet, but maybe we can find an angle." Paige frowns a little. "Taylor said the main reason she wants to do this is because Rhiannon is a good friend and she's been through some pretty tough times recently. Apparently her mom died before Christmas. Tragically, Taylor said, but she didn't go into details. Anyway, Rhiannon is depressed and Taylor thought an interview on our show might boost her spirits."

"I think it's a great idea," Fran says suddenly. "The angle is young creative hopefuls who are getting ready to work in the design world and what it takes to get them there. We can do a show following the Oscars Red Carpet show about this very thing. Maybe Rhiannon will know some other young designers to introduce us to, and maybe we can pick up some more back in LA."

"I like that," I say. "It might be inspiring to that viewer who's watching our show and maybe she thinks she'd like to get into design herself." I make a face at Paige. "Because *not everyone* is cut out to be a model."

Paige shrugs this off.

"But Erin is right. We need to expand the market and pull in as many viewers as possible, Paige. And a lot of girls are into design. We need to reach them too. Every fashion designer has to start somewhere. They aren't born as Marc Jacobs or Kate Spade—they work up to it."

Paige nods. "You're right. I think I could run with this. And it could make an interesting show." So she calls Taylor for Rhiannon's number, and then makes arrangements with Rhiannon to pop in on Monday morning. "I just want to meet you," Paige casually tells her after she introduces herself as a "friend of Taylor's" without giving her name. "And I'd like to see some of your designs and who knows ...?" Then she thanks her and says she'll see her next week.

"Does Rhiannon even get that this is a TV show?" I ask after Paige puts her phone away. The town car pulls up to the hotel entrance and the doorman is helping us out.

"No, I thought we could just surprise her with that."

"She'll still have to sign the waiver forms and everything," Fran says as we go into the lobby.

"We'll figure that out when the time comes."

We're just inside our suite when Paige's phone rings again. And this time she's even more excited. Sure, her voice is controlled and professional, but I can see her eyes glittering as she listens. "Yes, thank you," she says finally. "I'm looking forward to it. Yes, see you then. Thanks." Then she closes her phone and grabs me, letting out a squeal that makes my ears ring, and I'm wondering if security will be on their way up here.

"That was Dylan's assistant!"

"And?" I wait.

"And I've been invited to the *after party*."

"The after party?" I question. "After what?"

"After the show, you moron!"

"Wow." Fran nods as if this really is impressive. "Just you?"

"Sorry, that's all she said."

"That's okay," I say quickly. "I'm not into *after parties* anyway."

"Well, maybe I am." Fran frowns.

"I'm sorry, Fran." Paige puts her hand on Fran's shoulder. "You want me to call back and see if—"

"No, don't make me any more pathetic than I already sound." Fran laughs. "Good grief, I'll probably be fast asleep, and glad of it, by the time that party kicks into high gear."

"Me too." I nod.

"Not me," Paige grins as she dances around the living room of our suite. "I'm going to be having the time of my life."

"Just don't do anything stupid, okay?" I say. "I mean, you won't drink or anything, will you?"

"*Moi?*" She flutters her long eyelashes at me.

"*Paige.*" I put the warning in my voice and realize I sound a little like Mom.

"Oh, come on, one eensie-weensie-teensie glass of champagne won't hurt anything, will it?"

Fran frowns. "Paige," she says sternly, "Helen Hudson will have my head on a platter if you pull a Lindsay on us."

"Hey, Lindsay's doing okay these days."

"Yes, whatever. You know what I mean, Paige."

Paige holds her head high. "I plan to be very grown-up tonight."

"That's what worries me." Fran frowns at me now, like this is somehow my fault. "Erin, what would your mother say?"

I just shrug and suddenly feel tired. I wonder how I can sneak off to my bed to catch a few more winks, since we've been up since around five thirty and it's nearly one in the afternoon now.

"Well, I may not be your mother, but I know what I'm saying about this." It sounds like Fran is making an ultimatum and I pause to hear it.

"*What?*" Paige puts her hands on her hips with a worried brow.

"If you go, Erin goes."

"Wait a minute." I hold up my hands. "I don't want to—"

"This is about work, Erin. And you signed on with Paige to—"

"Why don't you go instead?" I plead.

Fran just laughs. "Yes, I'm sure they want to see an almost forty-year-old woman coming to—"

"You're almost forty?" Paige looks stunned.

"Well, I . . . uh, I exaggerated. Even so, if you go, Erin goes too, Paige. Do you understand?"

"But I—"

"Don't forget you're under contract." Fran holds her pointer finger out.

"*But they didn't invite Erin.*" Paige's voice is whiny now and she looks like she's about to go into pout mode.

"You're a smart girl. You know how these things work," Fran assures her. "It's not who you are, but who you know. Dylan wants you there, Erin is your sister. Trust me, they'll let her in too."

"Gee, thanks," I say. It's bad enough being forced to attend a party you don't want to, but to feel like you're extra baggage as well? Give me a break.

"And if they don't let Erin in, you'd better turn around and come back here ASAP," Fran tells her.

"If Erin *has* to come, she needs to look stylish. No way am I dragging in Camera Girl tonight. Forget it."

"I'm sure we can manage that." Fran is checking her phone now. "With all the clothes we're gathering up here, I think we might even be able to make me look stylish."

"You do look stylish," I tell her.

Fran smiles and thanks me, then tells me to hush as she says, "Hello, Helen. What's up?" Then she goes into a conversation about this week's film and edits and technical things that should interest me, and usually do, except that I feel like I'm falling asleep. And considering I might have a late night to look forward to, I'm going to really need this nap.

# Chapter 14

"Stand up straight," Paige commands me.

I comply, but I feel like screaming. "I don't really like this dress," I tell her. "I feel like I'm wearing a slip."

"You said that already," she tells me as she narrows her eyes, scrutinizing me from all angles.

"Yes, but you weren't listening."

"You're right," she concedes. "It does look like a slip." She picks up another dress from the bed. "I know Dylan is a fan of Valentino. Try this."

"Paige?" Luis is calling now. "Time to do your hair, sweetheart."

"And put on those red Prada pumps with it. Then come and show me," Paige calls as she hurries off to get her makeup done.

So I remove the slip-dress and put on the Valentino, which I don't even think is going to fit me since, according to the tag, it's one size too small. But it hugs me just right. I'm not sure if this line runs large or if I've lost some weight in our crazy run-around schedule, but when I look at it in the mirror, I'm surprised to see that the dress actually looks pretty good. It's mostly black, a heavy satin with red beaded trim. And it's elegant, yet understated. I'm not so sure about the red pumps, but when I put them on, they're obviously right. So I strut out to where Paige is getting her hair done and she lets out a happy squeal.

"Erin!" she cries. "You look awesome."

"Ooh-la-la," gushes Luis. "You look lovely."

JJ, our camera guy for tonight's suite shots, zooms in on me. And Fran comes over and nods with approval. "And you can be sure there will be press around tonight. You girls make sure to catch some of the action, okay?"

"I know just what to do with your hair," Luis says as he holds up his thumbs and forefingers as if to frame my face. "An updo. Definitely."

"Hey, Luis," calls Paige. "Remember me?"

He laughs and returns to the hair station he's set up in the living room. "Yes, my darling, you first."

"And I'll work on your makeup," Shauna says to me. "I'm thinking *red* lips, Erin. And I know you like the natural look, but tonight you are going for full glam, understand? So get out of that dress for now." And as if reading my mind, she adds, "And get over yourself."

"I've got the perfect coat for you to wear," Fran says as Shauna is working on my makeup. "It's a sweet little Kate Spade swing coat that she sent over the other day. And it'll be perfect with that dress and shoes."

And so when it's time to go, with JJ still shooting us, trying to get every angle, I feel almost as glamorous as Paige looks. Oh, I'm not delusional or anything. I know she looks absolutely fabulous. But I look pretty good too. Well, in a shorter, more compact, and more sensible way.

Paige is wearing Chanel—a perfectly cut sleeveless pink dress, trimmed in faux leopard, and topped with a matching coat that fits like it was made for her. The look is classy but sexy and totally Paige. Her hair is in a sleek French twist, her accessories are also Chanel, and her heels are faux-leopard Christian Louboutin. All are perfect.

"Will Dylan mind that you're not wearing his designs?" I ask as we go down the elevator. JJ has his camera down now so we can talk candidly.

"Of course not. Unless he's some kind of obsessed ego-maniac, and I really don't think that's the case."

JJ's camera comes back up as we walk through the lobby. But at least he's being discreet, and it's not like he's the only one with a camera. The lobby is packed—and getting more packed—as fashion fanatics pour through loaded down with bags, bags, and more bags.

Somehow Paige moves gracefully and effortlessly through the crowd and I try to imitate her. And I totally forget about JJ. After all, he's a pro; if he can't manage this, then there's no way I can help him. As we make our way outside to where our town car is supposed to be waiting, I can tell we're getting more than our fair share of looks. And once we're outside, we actually see some camera flashes. It's obvious that someone either knows who we are or thinks we're people he or she should know.

"Hold it," JJ says as we're about to enter the town car. "I want to get this shot."

The sidewalk and street are just as busy and noisy as the lobby and, once we're in the town car, it's obvious that traffic is snarled for blocks. I consider suggesting we just get out and walk, but these Pradas have very high heels and I'm worried I might trip and break something. Besides, we have plenty of time.

"This is kind of exciting," I tell Paige.

She smiles and nods. "Our first show of Fashion Week. Sure, there have already been a few shows today, but there's no way we can take them all in." I can tell she's talking for the sake of the camera now.

"It's hard to believe that Fashion Week can go on like this for a full week," I comment. "I mean, every day has around ten fashion shows, right?"

"By next Friday there will have been nearly a hundred shows."

"Wow." I shake my head. "I'm glad we're not going to all of them. It sounds exhausting."

"And if it makes you feel tired, think how the designers and their teams are feeling. Right now Dylan Marceau is probably on pins and needles."

"Maybe even literally," I add. "Those last-minute fixes and alterations."

"But Fashion Week will be over for Dylan Marceau as well as some other designers after tonight," Paige says. "Imagine what a relief it must be once your show is finished—and hopefully successful."

"Then you can just kick back and relax," I add, trying to play it up for the camera too.

"Of course, the price for this bit of relief is that designers like Dylan are the first ones out of the gates, while other designers still have up to eight days to see what the competition is like. And, you can bet that there'll be a lot of last-minute changes being made in the next few days—once they see what the other designers have done."

"Really? Do they worry that much about what the others are doing?"

Paige laughs. "Count on it. Fashion is a tough world. Spies are crawling all over these shows."

"With cameras?"

"Absolutely." She points toward JJ now. "That's why you need a press pass to be packing tonight."

JJ grins.

"Packing?" I frown. "A camera's not quite the same as a gun, Paige."

"It might be like that for a fashion designer. Their signature designs are their livelihood. If someone steals a design or upstages a designer, they might as well be packing a gun."

I kind of laugh. "That seems overly dramatic to me. But I do know it's a serious business."

"And an enormous industry." Paige begins tossing out some shockingly large figures. "It's not just the billions of dollars associated with the fashion industry—it represents a lot of jobs as well. Like you and me." She smiles. "And we take that seriously."

When we arrive at Bryant Park, it looks like a circus. The big tent is lit up and people and press are milling all over the place. JJ follows us with the camera as we make our way through the crowd. And when Paige spots someone with any kind of celebrity, she pauses to say hello—and if they're willing, she does a quick chat as JJ films.

Finally we are seated inside the tent. Front row! JJ is in the back with the rest of the press. For once, I'm not longing to be back there with them. Tonight I'm enjoying this. Tonight I'm perfectly happy being a fashionista sitting front row on the first night of Fashion Week.

Dylan's show begins with Taylor Mitchell striding out in a brown velvet ensemble of fitted pants and a gorgeous jacket. At the end of the runway, she gracefully removes the flowing jacket to reveal a gold satin blouse beneath. The belt, accessories, boots — all is perfection. And the crowd shows their approval with applause. Model after model comes out, quickly making her way up and down the runway, never missing a beat. And each outfit is fantastic. Okay, maybe not clothes I'd be comfortable in, but not over-the-top either. And I've learned enough about design to know that runway fashion is not the same as off-the-rack fashion. These clothes are a dramatized exaggeration of what will be available to retailers soon, but even still, as I watch this show I'm thinking Dylan Marceau might be my favorite designer. Sure, some of his outfits, like the peacock cocktail dress with feathers everywhere, are a little weird, but a lot of them could be fun to wear. All in all, I can only assume that his show is a success. When he finally emerges, to thundering applause, walking the runway with Taylor at his side, it's obvious that he's pleased.

Paige manages to get some of the models, including Taylor, in front of the camera as she discusses their outfits. I mostly just watch, wondering how my sister manages to come up with so many questions and comments without ever sounding redundant.

"Okay," she says to JJ. "I think we've got enough, don't you?"

He nods and lowers his camera. "Unless you want me to come with you to the after party."

Paige just laughs. "No, thank you."

"Then I'll head outside and see what kind of candid spots

I can catch."

"Great idea."

"And I told Fran I'd meet up with her at the salon," he adds. "She thought she might be able to get a press pass."

The after party is at a nearby hotel, but when I call for our town car, the driver tells me that traffic is too jammed to get through. "It'll be at least an hour to get in," he explains, "and it could be another hour to get you to the hotel." I ask him to hold, then relay this to Paige.

"Two hours to go like eight blocks?"

I just nod.

She frowns. "I guess we'll just have to hoof it."

I look down at my red Pradas, which are already starting to make my feet ache. I cannot imagine walking eight New York blocks right now. "Are you sure?"

"What else can we do?"

"A cab?" I nod over to where a number of cabs are lined up.

"Those are either engaged or waiting. And even if we got one, they would be stuck in traffic too."

I shake my head. "Next time I'm bringing some walking shoes to change into."

"That's not a bad idea. Well, unless a camera catches us. That wouldn't be too pretty." Paige points toward 42nd Street. "That way."

We've only gone a block and I know I won't make it in these shoes. I'm about to beg Paige to call for our town car even if it does mean an hour-long wait, but then I see a street vendor who is selling, among other things, rubber flip-flops. I practically run to him, opening my purse and happily plunking down fifteen dollars for footwear that's probably worth two bucks. Paige laughs at me as I do a quick shoe switch.

But she's not laughing seven blocks later when she starts complaining that her feet are now screaming at her.

It's nearly nine o'clock when we make it to the hotel, but Paige doesn't want to go up to the party yet. "It's probably barely even started," she tells me.

"I don't care," I protest. "I just want to sit down and put my feet up."

"Let's go use the restroom, freshen up, and get a coffee first." She frowns at my flip-flops. "And get rid of those things before someone sees us."

So I comply with Paige's wishes, but instead of dumping the flip-flops like Paige wants, I hide them behind the trash can just in case I need them later. We manage to kill more time drinking coffee and I even have the foresight to call and ask for the town car to pick us up at midnight, although Paige insists that's too early.

Finally it's 9:45 and Paige thinks it's okay to go up. As it turns out, she was right. The party does seem to be just beginning as people are trickling in. But Paige immediately finds someone and starts chatting and schmoozing—almost as if she thinks she's on camera still—while I try not to look too awkward as I stand beside her. We continue to move around, "working the room," as she says. And, although I'm tired and just want to kick back a little, I soon realize there aren't too many places left to sit. The few chairs available are near people significantly older than I am, so I know I'll look like a serious party pooper if I join them.

It doesn't take long to figure out that this party is mostly about being seen. I notice there are a few cameras here and I wonder why we didn't have JJ come too. After an hour or so, Dylan spots us and waves. Then, to my surprise, he comes right over. He takes Paige's hands in his and they exchange air kisses as she congratulates him on his show. And then, to my huge relief, he invites us to join him at his table, where there are *chairs.*

Champagne is flowing and I don't throw a hissy fit when Paige accepts a glass. And to show I'm a good sport, I accept a glass too. But I mostly just pretend to sip it. I really don't like the taste anyway.

"Hey, everyone," says Taylor Mitchell as she and two other beautiful girls come to our table. "Room for more?"

"Always for you girls," Dylan tells her. Then he waves to one of the waiters, asking him to round up three more chairs.

"This is my best friend, DJ," Taylor says as they sit down with us. "Her grandmother is Katherine Carter—"

"You're Katherine Carter's granddaughter!" Paige exclaims as she shakes DJ's hand. "You're a professional model too, right?"

DJ kind of shrugs. "Not really. I mean, I've done some work, but I'm mostly a student now."

"We're trying to talk her into coming back to New York this summer," Taylor says. "She has no problem finding work."

"And you don't want to do that?" Paige looks shocked.

DJ looks uncomfortable now, like this isn't really her thing. I think maybe I can relate to this girl. Then Taylor introduces us to her roommate, Eliza Wilton.

"And you're a model too." Paige smiles at her.

"I am for now," Eliza says lightly. "I hear you girls are going to stay with us for a day or two after Fashion Week."

Paige talks a bit about our show now and what she'd like to accomplish when we're at their apartment. "Kind of a day in the life of a model sort of thing," she says finally. And then they're all talking about Dylan's brilliant show tonight and congratulating him on his fall lineup. I realize that DJ, who's sitting next to me, doesn't seem to be fully engaged in this conversation. Of course, I'm not either.

"So, let me guess," I say to her. "You're not as into fashion as Taylor and Eliza?"

She laughs. "Is it that obvious?"

"Maybe it's just that I can relate."

She looks curiously at me. "You're not into it either? What about your TV show?"

I shake my head. "I'm doing that for my sister's sake. Anyway, mostly I signed on to be the camera girl." I make a face. "That was the producer's idea. A way to get both of us on the show. A sister act, you know."

"Very clever."

"The truth is I'm really much more interested in photography." Then I tell her about UCLA and how it was hard to give it up in exchange for the show.

"That's exactly how I feel about school. Taylor didn't want me to leave New York last fall, but by the end of summer I was so sick of fashion and modeling, I couldn't wait to get back to a normal life."

"That's how I feel a lot of the time. But I have to admit I'm getting some good experience. I even got to shoot all the footage when we did Dylan's studio. It was pretty fun."

DJ and I talk some more and I learn that she attends a small college in Connecticut and that she has a boyfriend. I also learn that both she and Taylor are Christians, and can't help but be a little stunned.

"That surprises you?" she asks.

"Well, I just didn't expect to discover too many believers

in the fashion industry."

"That's kind of true. But Taylor is sincere in her faith. And I think she's making an impression. She'll talk to anyone about God and most of the time, people listen. It's really cool."

I nod. "Definitely."

We continue to talk and I realize that I really like this girl. She's grounded and smart and, like me, she takes her faith seriously. Finally, the party seems to be winding down and Taylor and her friends are getting ready to leave, which I use as a cue to get Paige to go too.

"Are you going to be at Taylor's when we come to stay?" Paige asks DJ as we're going down the elevator together.

"No, I'll be back at school."

"I could barely talk her into coming for Dylan's show," Taylor admits. "In fact, I had to get her grandmother involved."

DJ laughs. "Yes, Taylor enticed my grandmother to come for the Ralph Lauren show tomorrow, then used that to get me to commit to come too."

"So, we'll see you tomorrow then," Paige says as we go into the lobby.

"Grandmother and I will be there," DJ promises. "Front row seats."

"Mrs. Carter is an old friend of Ralph Lauren," Eliza explains.

"Mrs. Carter is an old friend of almost anyone in the fashion industry," Taylor adds. "Well, unless they're too new. Although, Dylan is new and she somehow connected with him."

"Well, I would love to meet Mrs. Carter," Paige says. "Do you think she'd be willing to be on our show?"

DJ laughs. "Are you kidding?"

Taylor nods. "Oh, yeah, you won't have to twist her arm

much."

"And the old girl can tell some stories," Eliza adds.

So we part ways, and to my relief our town car has made it through traffic and is outside waiting for us. And although the streets are still clogged with taxis and limos and town cars, we manage to make it to our hotel before one. And, really, the after party turned out to be better than expected—and getting to know Taylor and DJ was the best part.

# Chapter
## 15

The Ralph Lauren show is also in the tent, but this time it's an afternoon show. This time I think to pack a pair of walking shoes in my oversized bag. And since it's an afternoon event — with no after party — we dress a bit more casually. At least I do, wearing pants today. Paige still looks like she could be meeting the queen in a sleek navy dress and matching coat along with navy and white spectator pumps — all Prada. But unless there's a beach or a picnic involved, Paige rarely does casual.

After the show, which is very good, Fran gets an idea. "Let's invite Mrs. Carter and anyone else who's free to come to lunch with us," she suggests. Everyone is milling around now, chatting and doing closer inspections of the models' outfits. Fran nods to Paige as she's reaching for her phone. "I'll see what I can set up while you girls go talk to Mrs. Carter and her granddaughter."

Paige and I work our way through the crowd to where Mrs. Carter, a white-haired woman dressed impeccably in a pale blue suit with a striped pastel scarf draped around her neck, seems to be holding court with a small group of fashion freaks. Okay, I'm trying not to think in such negative terms, but it does get overwhelming.

As she's talking, Mrs. Carter seems to notice Paige and smiles directly at her, then waves us to come over and join her. DJ introduced us before the show, and I could tell Mrs. Carter was interested in our TV series.

"Paige Forrester," Mrs. Carter calls out, "come over here, darling. You and your sister. I'd like you to meet some friends." And just like that, we're being introduced to the current editor-in-chief of *Couture* and a couple of editors from other fashion magazines. I'm thinking this would've been a great scene to include in our show and that it's too bad we didn't have a press pass to allow some of our crew in here. Or even me with my camera. But at least JJ is outside, waiting for us. Paige kept him busy for much of the morning doing spots with anyone who seemed interested in getting face time on TV.

"I know this is very last minute," Paige jumps in after the editors have moved along. "But we wondered if you and DJ might like to join us for lunch, Mrs. Carter."

"That sounds delightful," she tells her. "I already made a reservation at our hotel, but I asked for a large table just in case I ran into friends today. I'd be happy to share it if that works for you." Then she tells us the name of the hotel—it's the same one we're staying in.

"You're welcome to ride with us," Paige offers, "but our camera guy will be along too. So, unless you're opposed to being on our show, there could be some filming."

Mrs. Carter laughs. "Well, if you can stand to have my old face on your show, I'm happy to oblige."

"I have so many questions for you," Paige bubbles. "You're such a fashion icon and you know everything and everybody."

Mrs. Carter waves her hand, but I suspect she's flattered. DJ actually winks at me, as if to indicate that her grandmother is eating this up. And before long we're loaded into the limo, and JJ is sitting across from Paige and Mrs. Carter as they have what seems like just a casual and candid conversation while they're leaving the Ralph Lauren show.

Paige asks the standard questions about Mrs. Carter's background, her years as a professional model, and her position as editor-in-chief at *Couture*.

"Yes, I had thought I was retired," Mrs. Carter says as she reaches for her granddaughter's hand. "But then Desiree's — I mean DJ's, she doesn't really like being called Desiree ... As I was saying, DJ's mother was killed in a car accident and DJ came to live with me. I saw this gorgeous young girl and I knew that she had real model potential. Not just because she is tall and pretty, but she has the bone structure and, when she stands up straight, the posture and stance. And I knew this girl could really be something."

DJ laughs so loudly that she snorts. "Except for the small hitch that *this girl* didn't really want to be a model."

"That's true." Mrs. Carter nods sadly, as if she's still getting over this. "But I do understand. DJ marches to her own drummer and that's okay. She's a wonderful granddaughter and I couldn't be prouder of her."

"But you had other girls living in your home too, is that right?" Paige continues.

"Yes. Because of my hopes to groom DJ into — well, you know how that went. And because some other situations arose where other teenage girls had a need for housing, and I had this overly large Victorian home in Connecticut ... well, it just seemed to fall into place. So a couple of years ago, I took five other young women into my home."

"You had six teenage girls under one roof?" Paige looks shocked.

Mrs. Carter laughs. "It's true. I had no idea what I was getting into." Mrs. Carter and DJ take turns regaling us with wild tales of the goings on at Carter House and how the Carter House girls made quite a name for themselves in the local high school. It's good entertainment. And it makes the hour-long car ride (through snail's-pace traffic) pass quickly.

The stories continue on through lunch, only now I'm the one behind the camera—attempting to be discreet as I capture this conversation, which Fran is hoping might fill up an entire episode of *On the Runway*. Then, just as we're considering dessert and coffee, Taylor joins us, and the stories not only continue, but become much more colorful too. It ends up being a three-hour lunch, but as we're heading off to our rooms, it seems that we've all enjoyed it.

On Sunday morning, we do the Marc Jacobs show. This time, our camera guys have press passes and Paige manages to get some pretty hot off-the-cuff interviews, which pleases Fran immensely.

Then on Monday morning it's cold and drizzly and we get in our town car and head over to a small studio on the edge of the garment district, apparently owned by a designer who's not having a show for Fashion Week, and there we meet Rhiannon Farley. We already know that Rhiannon is a former Carter House girl and that she is much loved by DJ,

Taylor, and Mrs. Carter. We also know that Rhiannon wants to be a designer and that her mother recently died of a drug overdose.

Rhiannon is the one who lets us into the studio, explaining that she's the only one here today. "The others are trying to take in as much of Fashion Week as possible."

"Did we keep you from that?" Paige asks as we go inside.

"No, not really. I mean, I'll go to some of the shows — our school gets passes and we're expected to attend. But I hadn't planned to go to all of them. It's too overwhelming, not to mention impossible." Rhiannon looks at us with a puzzled brow and I can tell she wonders why we're here.

"I'm sorry," Paige says quickly to recover. Then she goes into a brief introduction and asks if it's okay for me to use my camera.

Rhiannon still looks confused. "Why?"

Paige reaches in her pocket and hands Rhiannon a card. "I forgot to mention that we're from — "

"*On the Runway?*" Rhiannon's jaw literally drops. "I've heard of this show and I've been wanting to see it, but I don't have a TV in my dorm room. Are you *really* from this show?"

Paige smiles and nods. "And if it's okay with you, Erin will begin filming until the camera crew arrives. We'd like to do an episode about young designers and what it takes to make it, and we want to feature you."

"Me?" Rhiannon looks stunned. "Why?"

"Because we've heard you're really talented." Paige explains what Taylor and Mrs. Carter had said, and then Fran gets Rhiannon to sign the release form. But I can tell she's still shocked by all this, and I'm wondering if it would've been better to give this poor girl some warning. I mean, what if she wore an outfit she hates today? Although she looks great in her short plaid skirt, black tights, and a lacy white blouse, which I'm guessing might be one of her own creations.

As my camera rolls, I'm trying to capture Rhiannon's surprised delight as she continues to absorb what's really going on, but I wish she'd relax a little. It's as if her words and movements are guarded, like she can't let down in front of us.

As I focus the camera on her I realize that she's much shorter than Paige, and although she's very pretty with her long, curly auburn hair and green eyes, she doesn't seem like the model type. I mean that as a compliment. But she also doesn't seem very comfortable (like me) while the camera's on her. Paige asks Rhiannon some routine questions, and I can tell she's trying to get Rhiannon to relax.

When the crew finally arrives I make room for them, but I continue to film Rhiannon as she gives us a quick tour of the small studio. Soon, she's talking about her own designs and what she hopes to achieve, and it's like she's suddenly coming to life.

"I want to be a responsible designer," she says as she holds up an absolutely beautiful dress that's a combination of all kinds of fabrics and notions and things. It's kind of a like a patchwork creation, and yet it's elegant and graceful-looking in varying shades of purple. "I try to use materials that are organic, recycled, and renewable … and I try to make each garment one of a kind."

"Similar to Granada Greenwear's mission," Paige suggests. "Although I must say your styles are completely different. Perhaps more feminine."

Rhiannon nods. "I adore Granada Greenwear. But, yes, I'd agree, our styles are different."

"Your designs have a very delicate quality to them," Paige says as she holds up a sky-blue dress. "Almost fairy-like."

Rhiannon laughs and her eyes sparkle. "Yes, I've heard that before."

"This is beautiful," Paige says as she continues to study the blue dress. "I usually go more for the classic contemporary styles, but I think I would wear something like this ... if it were the right occasion." She nods to the rack of other clothes. "Why don't you show us some more? Tell us about what you were hoping for with each creation, and what inspires you."

It's like Paige has somehow managed to flick the switch and Rhiannon comes completely and totally to life. I can tell that this interview is not only going well, but it will look fantastic on film too.

After more than an hour, we finally wind it down. But then Paige gets an idea. "How would you feel if I try on that gorgeous blue dress?" she asks Rhiannon. "To get some footage of it for the show. Is that all right?"

"Are you kidding?" Rhiannon rushes to the get the dress, thrusting it toward Paige. "I would love that!"

So while Paige is changing into the dress and Rhiannon scrambles to find the shoes that she knows will be perfect, we get our cameras ready to roll again. When Paige announces she's coming out, we are filming. She pushes open the curtains and, not like a striding model but more like a ballerina, she glides out of the fitting room and sort of dances around the studio. "This dress is absolutely amazing," she says. "I feel almost magical in it. Like I could do ballet or a very lovely waltz." Then she goes and stands next to Rhiannon. "I'm Paige Forrester from *On the Runway*, standing next to a young woman who I'm certain is going to become a well-known designer before long. And I am wearing one of her dresses—an original Rhiannon Farley creation. And I am loving it." She holds out a foot to show a delicate old-fashioned-looking ballerina slipper that's encrusted with beads, buttons, and other things. "Don't forget to put your best foot forward, and today it's a Rhiannon creation. See you next week!"

"Cut," calls Fran. "That's a wrap."

Rhiannon hugs Paige. "Thank you so much." She actually has tears in her eyes. "You have no idea what this has meant to me." She fumbles to find a scrap of cloth that she uses to blot her tears. "Even if it doesn't make it on your show, I'm still—"

"Oh, don't kid yourself," Fran is telling Rhiannon. "I have no doubt this is going to make it on our show. It's one of the most unique and refreshing interviews we've done."

Rhiannon thanks everyone now. Then she turns to Paige. "Please, keep the dress."

"Keep it?" Paige says lightly. "I already planned to buy it, if that's okay."

"No, I want to give it to you."

"But I want to—"

Rhiannon holds up her forefinger to stop her. "No. You must let me give it to you. I have this very strong feeling—a spiritual feeling—that I need to give it to you. So please let me."

Paige smiled. "Only if you let me buy the shoes."

Rhiannon sticks out her hand. "It's a deal."

Then we tell Rhiannon about how we're going to stay with Taylor and Eliza after Fashion Week ends. And I ask if she might be able to pop over while we're there. "It'd be fun to get to know you better."

"Are you kidding? I'd love to come."

So, feeling like we're all old friends, Paige and I both hug

Rhiannon, and then we head back to our hotel. And I have to say, I don't think I've enjoyed doing a segment for a show as much as the one we did today. Rhiannon is a cool girl. And seeing her response to being on our show gives me hope — like maybe there's more going on with *On the Runway* than I ever realized.

Later the same afternoon, we attend another designer's show. And although this guy is an amazing designer, I keep mentally comparing him to Rhiannon and, well, it's like comparing apples and stardust.

Then on Tuesday we see Kate Spade's show and afterward we meet Helen for dinner. She tells us that she's seen footage from last week and that she's feeling very hopeful. "You girls were right to make this an extended trip in New York. It's going to be worth the extra expense."

We all go to the Perry Ellis show on Wednesday afternoon and then to Badgley Mischka on Thursday morning. The final show for Paige and me is Miu Miu on Friday afternoon — and I think if I never see another fashion show, it will be too soon.

# Chapter

## 16

*"How are you holding up?" Blake asks me* over the phone on Saturday afternoon. Paige and I have finally made it to the FIT museum, which has turned out to be rather interesting. We're both particularly intrigued with the sixties and seventies section. I'm not even sure why.

"I'm doing okay now," I tell him as I take a sip of coffee. Paige and I are taking a little break and checking our phones.

"So were the fashion shows pretty great?"

"I guess so. But you know me, a little bit of fashion goes a long way." Then I tell him about our interview with Rhiannon.

"And she's only twenty?"

"Yes. But she seems a lot older. I think it's because she's kind of been taking care of herself—she must've grown up fast. But she's friends with Taylor Mitchell and she's going to join our little slumber party tonight."

"It's tonight?"

"Yeah—we decided to change it so that both Rhiannon and DJ could be there. I guess it's kind of a Carter House reunion, except two of the girls aren't coming. One goes to Harvard and the other one lives in California."

"So you and Paige are their replacements?" He chuckles. "And you *will* get all this on film, right? I know I'd like to see it."

"That's pretty much the idea, and it should be interesting. But we told the camera guys they can only stay until midnight. And then we'll regroup with just Taylor and Eliza on Tuesday for a slice of the model life in New York City."

"And then back home on Wednesday?"

"That's the plan."

"So . . . you'll be home for Valentine's Day."

I consider this. "Yeah, that's about a week away, right?"

"Uh-huh."

So now I'm wondering, what's going on? Why did he bring this up?

"I thought maybe you'd want to do something . . . something with me."

"You mean like a date?"

"I know . . . you don't want to get serious."

I don't say anything. I'm not really sure what to say. And I'm not really sure how I feel either. The truth is I think it might be fun to go out with Blake again—on a real date. But at the same time, I'm not sure.

"Let me guess," he says, "you're trying to think of a way to let me down gently. Right?"

"No . . . not at all."

"Really?"

"I was just thinking. That's all."

"Thinking?"

"I don't know. I mean, going on a date doesn't *have* to mean we're serious, does it? Can't a date just be a date?"

"Yeah, sure. Why not?"

"If we understand this up front ... I don't see why we couldn't go out."

"On Valentine's Day?" He sounds skeptical.

"Well, as long as you don't try to turn it into some big romantic thing."

"So, what do you think? Wanna go bowling?"

I laugh. "Well, it doesn't have to be *that* unromantic."

"Maybe I think bowling is romantic."

"Fine," I say. "Let's go bowling."

"How about we just keep that on the options list."

"Sounds good."

"Well, you girls have fun at your slumber party. I wouldn't mind being a fly on that wall—all these gorgeous girls sitting around in their pajamas talking about ... hey, what *will* you talk about?"

"Since Paige will probably take charge, and since almost everyone there is into fashion big-time, I'll let you guess."

"Poor Erin."

"Nah, I'll be okay." Then I tell him about how Taylor and DJ are Christians. "And I have a feeling Rhiannon might be too. I don't know about Eliza though. She's a little hard to read, but I get the impression this girl is from money. Especially since her parents are footing the bill on the apartment, which sounds pretty swanky."

"Sounds interesting to me."

We wind down the conversation and, after I hang up, I think maybe it does sound interesting. But by the time I drop my phone in my bag, Paige is getting worried. She insists we need to head back to the hotel and get ourselves *ready* for the big slumber party.

"It's just a slumber party," I say as we ride back in the town car. "What's there to get ready for?"

Paige presses her lips together like she's thinking. "I guess I mean mentally ready."

"Mentally ready for a slumber party?"

"Well, you know the cameras will be running."

"Right."

"And I'll be expected to keep the conversation interesting. And, well, I remember from when I was younger how it can get at a slumber party."

"What do you mean?" I'm trying to remember, but mostly what I can recall is just a lot of talking, eating junk food, watching weird movies, laughing, and staying up too late. I don't see the big deal.

"You know how girls can be at a slumber party."

"You mean like in middle school?"

She shrugs, but I have a feeling there's something she's not telling me.

"What?" I persist. "Did something happen to you at a slumber party?"

She shrugs again.

"What happened, Paige?"

"Well, it was a long time ago."

"Tell me."

She frowns. "It's not important." But I urge her and finally she pours it out. "I'm not sure if it was premeditated or if it just happened, but it was McKenzie's fourteenth birthday and for some reason she decided to target me. She kept kind of jabbing at me, making fun of my outfit, making fun of how I was into fashion, making fun of everything . . . and since it was her birthday and her party . . . well, the other girls ... even my best friend Kelsey joined in. I finally just left."

"Was that the time you had Mom pick you up in the middle of the night?"

"Yeah." She nods sadly. "I couldn't take it. They just got meaner and meaner. It was really brutal."

"I thought it was because you were having cramps."

"That's what I told Mom. No way was I going to admit to her that I'd been the girl that everyone had turned on. It was so pathetic. But I guess it still hurts."

"I can understand."

So, a couple hours later, when we're going up in the elevator to Taylor and Eliza's fifteenth-floor apartment, I try to be as upbeat and positive as I can. And I assure Paige that middle-school mean girls are a thing of the past. Of course, even as I say this, I'm recalling another mean-girl incident — and it had nothing to do with middle school, but instead the cast members of *Malibu Beach*.

As expected our camera crew is already there and JJ is set up to film us as we emerge from the elevator with our overnight bags. Then we are mic'ed and Paige makes a smooth transition into what we're doing tonight and who we expect to see.

"Just girls visiting with girls," she says lightly. "Letting our hair down after a long eight days of Fashion Week." Then she rings the doorbell and within seconds, Taylor warmly welcomes us into their beautiful apartment, where the rest of the crew is already set up and rolling. Taylor explains that DJ is picking up Rhiannon and that they should be here in about an hour. "And I know it sounds juvenile, but I ordered pizza. I hope that's okay."

"A model who eats pizza?" I ask.

Taylor laughs. "Yes. Eliza wasn't too happy with that decision. She's been on a pretty strict diet lately."

"Where is Eliza?" Paige asks.

Taylor nods toward a partially closed door. "Primping, of course."

"I am *not* primping," Eliza calls back.

Taylor gets us sodas, and is giving us a quick tour of the plush apartment when Eliza finally makes her entrance. I have to agree with Taylor, I think she was primping. Her makeup is perfect. Her hair is perfect. Although she has on warm-ups, they too are perfect—pale blue and about the same color as her eyes. In fact, I think Paige might have the exact same ones.

"I was just getting comfortable," Eliza says as she grabs herself a diet soda then gracefully arranges herself on the sectional—as if she's striking a pose for a leisure wear ad. Or maybe it's a jewelry ad, because she's wearing diamonds. I can tell she's aware of the cameras, and I suspect JJ and Alistair can tell too.

"This is a beautiful apartment," Paige tells Eliza as she sits in a chair adjacent from her, crossing one long blue-jeaned leg over the other and showing off her new pair of Prada boots.

"Thank you." Eliza makes a blasé look. "But it's my mother's decorator who should take the credit. Lamar is a magician when it comes to making small spaces seem larger."

"This seems like a fairly big apartment." Paige observes. "For Manhattan anyway. And I'm guessing most models don't have digs quite this posh."

"The successful ones do," Eliza says in a slightly arrogant tone.

"So, is that how you'd describe your career?"

Eliza's smile stiffens. "Oh, I don't know."

"How about you, Taylor?" Paige turns her attention to Taylor as she sits down next to her roommate. "How would you describe your career so far?"

"Interesting ... challenging ... fun." Taylor picks up a copy of *Vogue* and starts to flip through it.

"What's your favorite part about modeling?" Paige asks her.

Taylor considers this. "Maybe the go-sees."

"Go sees?" I echo.

She nods. "That's when your agency gives you a call, saying that someone — you know, a designer or a photographer working on a print ad — wants you to stop by so they can check you out and go over your portfolio. It's called a *go-see*."

"As in go see if they like you," Eliza adds.

"And then it's a callback if they do," Taylor tells me.

"How about you, Eliza?" Paige asks. "Are go-sees your favorite part too?"

"No way." Eliza shakes her head firmly.

"Why not?"

"Too stressful."

Paige turns back to Taylor. "So why do you like go-sees?"

Taylor's dark eyes seem to spark at this question. And I think it's no wonder she's such a sought-after model. "It's like a challenge, you know? Kind of like taking a test so you can prove that you're good at something. I think it's fun to walk in cold and suddenly you have to win these people over. Kind of like a game. If DJ were here — she's into sports — I think she'd get it. It's like a contest and you want to win. Does that make sense?"

Paige nods with enthusiasm. "Absolutely. In fact, that's exactly how I feel when I walk into an interview situation. I have no idea how it's going to go down, but I can't wait to get started. It is kind of like a game too."

"I get that," I tell them. "It's kind of like that for me when I'm trying to get a good shot on my camera. It's exciting."

"Like it stirs up your passion," Taylor continues. "It energizes you and you want to do your best."

"How about you, Eliza?" Paige tries again to include her. "What is it about modeling that feels like that to you?"

Eliza frowns as if she's trying to think of something, and then she just slowly shakes her head. "I'm not really sure."

"But you do like modeling?" Paige tries.

"I love it."

"So what about it do you love?"

"I guess it's the actual doing. You know, striding down the runway. Or if it's for print, posing for the camera. I love to be the center of attention."

Taylor laughs. "That's the truth."

"Well, so do you," Eliza shoots back.

"Yeah, I suppose you're right. But it's more than just that."

"Which do you like better?" Paige continues. "Runway or print?"

"Both," Taylor admits.

Eliza nods. "Yes. I like both too."

Paige continues to quiz these two girls about the modeling life and Eliza seems to relax a little, as if she's forgetting the camera crew is there.

And then DJ and Rhiannon arrive with the pizzas and the place gets much livelier—and crowded. Paige continues to keep the conversation fashion-oriented, and the banter and chat is animated and fun. But after an hour or so, Paige suggests that the camera crew might want to call it a night.

"We'll see you again on Monday," JJ tells Taylor as they're leaving. And I can tell by the way he smiles at her that he's looking forward to coming back.

And then it's just the six of us and Paige sets aside her interviewer mode and just acts like one of the girls. But something weird is happening. It's like Eliza has decided she doesn't like Paige.

"So how did you manage to land this TV job anyway?" Eliza asks Paige. She's been quizzing her about *On the Runway*, but in a way that sounds like a putdown. "Did you just sleep with the right guy?" She laughs like this is funny.

"Well, Helen Hudson spotted Paige when she was doing a news spot for Channel Five News," I explain. "Helen said that Paige has what it takes to do a show like *On the Runway*. Helen called and set up the interview, and that was that."

"So what if your show doesn't really take off?" Eliza asks. "Do you have some kind of backup plan? Any other aspirations?"

"Nothing specifically," Paige tells her. "But I'm hoping whatever I do will be fashion-related. And who knows ... maybe one thing will lead to another."

"Have you ever considered modeling?" Rhiannon asks Paige. "I mean, you seem like a natural."

"Thanks." Paige smiles at her. "But I don't think I'd really want to model. To me it's more fun *talking* about fashion. Besides, unless you're a Kate Moss, Heidi Klum, or Tyra Banks, a model's career doesn't usually last too long." Paige turns to Eliza. "How about you? Do you have any aspirations beyond modeling? Or a backup plan if it doesn't work out for you?"

"Besides your family's fortune," DJ says teasingly.

Eliza scowls. "I promised my parents I'd go to college

after I'm done modeling. Not that I'm planning to do that anytime soon."

"How about you?" Eliza asks Taylor.

"It might be fun to get into acting." Taylor kicks off her shoes and tucks her legs beneath her. "Once the modeling thing dries up."

"Not that Taylor's modeling career will dry up any time soon," DJ adds. "Did she tell you the good news?"

"What good news?" Paige asks with interest.

DJ nods to Taylor. "You didn't tell them?"

Taylor just shrugs.

"*Couture* has chosen Taylor to be in their next editorial fashion spread," DJ tells everyone. "Isn't that great?"

"Seriously?" Eliza looks shocked. "When did this happen?"

"Grandmother told me about it," DJ explains. "Apparently the editor-in-chief thought Taylor was the hottest thing during Fashion Week."

"That's probably an exaggeration," Taylor says.

"And I'm guessing Mrs. Carter suggested it," Eliza says to Paige. "You know she used to be editor-in-chief at *Couture*. I'm sure she still carries some influence there. Plus, she always did tend to favor Taylor over the rest of us."

"I wouldn't say that," DJ challenges. "She might've thought Taylor had the most potential for modeling, but she recognized talents in others too."

Eliza just laughs—but in a mean way.

"She encouraged me toward design," Rhiannon says. "And helped me get into FIT."

"Hey, I have an idea," Paige says suddenly. "How about if we take Tuesday's *On the Runway* shoot over to *Couture*?"

"That's a great idea," I tell her.

"What do you think, Taylor?" Paige asks.

"Wouldn't you need to ask *Couture* what they think first?" Eliza says sharply, cutting off Taylor.

But Paige is already on her phone, calling Fran and telling her about this idea. She explains how Taylor has been chosen for the editorial fashion spread and how that would make a great angle for the day in the life of a model episode, then finally hangs up. "Fran loves this idea," Paige tells us. "She's all over it. And I'm guessing *Couture* will be too. After all, it's free publicity for them."

"So your day in the life of a model is basically turning into a day in the life of Taylor Mitchell," Eliza says sullenly.

"We'll include you too," Paige assures her.

"Yeah, right." Eliza stands and goes into the kitchen. And I'm sure her feelings are hurt, but it also seems like she's being pretty selfish. Why can't she be happy for Taylor's sake?

"Now don't go off and pout," DJ calls to Eliza. "We all know you're feeling jealous of Taylor. Nothing new about this." DJ turns to Paige and me. "Living in the same house for a year, we started acting a little like sisters."

"Come on, Eliza," Rhiannon now tries. "You can talk to us about what's bugging you."

So Eliza returns, flops down on the sectional again, and just shakes her head. "It seems like no matter how hard I try, it just never goes quite the way I want it to."

"Maybe it's because you want the wrong things," I say hesitantly.

"Good point," Rhiannon adds.

"How do you know what's right or wrong for me?" Eliza challenges.

"I guess I don't," I admit. "But you seem unhappy to me. And that makes me wonder if you're heading the wrong way."

"So you're saying that the things I want are wrong?" Eliza points to Paige now. "I mean, you get to be the star of your own show." She points to Taylor. "And you're turning out to be a supermodel." She points to Rhiannon. "You're getting to design like you wanted." Then she points to DJ and just frowns. "You don't even try and you always seem to land on top."

"That's not true," DJ tells her.

"But no matter what I do or how hard I work, I'm always getting beat out by someone else. It's just not fair."

"Maybe God is trying to tell you something," DJ says quietly.

Eliza just rolls her eyes. "Here comes the sermon."

"Maybe you should listen to the sermon," Taylor tells her. "It might answer some of your questions."

"Because you're living an Eliza-directed life," DJ points out. "And you're going after what Eliza wants without any regard for what God might have for you."

"And what God has for you is so much more," Rhiannon adds.

"I agree," I say cautiously. "I'm trying to live a God-directed life too. And I'm not saying I do everything right, because I definitely don't. But I try to trust God and I pray for him to show me what's best for me. And, right now, I'm getting to do this TV show with Paige—which by the way, wasn't something that I originally wanted to do. But the more I do it, the more I realize that God wants me to be with my sister ... to help her in whatever way I can."

Paige gives me a tolerant smile. "I'm sure God knows just how desperately I need your help too."

"But I'm not the star of the show," I say to Eliza, "and that's just fine with me. I wouldn't even want to be the star. For me it's more fun helping someone else to shine."

Rhiannon nods. "That's how I feel too. I mean, I love to design, but the really cool part is watching someone else wearing the clothes I made. Not everyone can be the star. At least not all the time."

"But I *want* to be the star!" Eliza insists. "Why is that wrong?"

"Maybe God doesn't want you to be the star," I suggest. "Maybe he has a different, better kind of plan for your life."

"But how will you know if you don't ask him?" DJ adds.

We talk about this for about an hour and although Eliza can't seem to let go of wanting stardom, I think maybe she's considering what we're trying to tell her. And I think maybe Paige is too. Because in some ways, Paige and Eliza are similar, except that I think Paige's motivation is about more than just being a star. She genuinely loves what she's doing. And I'm guessing that's why it's working for her.

# Chapter 17

On Monday, we return to Taylor and Eliza's apartment in time to see them getting up in the morning and having breakfast, although Eliza barely eats and Paige makes a comment about it, which makes Eliza mad. Then after they're dressed and ready for the day, we head out, tagging along as they go to the modeling agency.

"I know it's more than your typical day," Fran tells them as we ride in the town car, "but viewers will appreciate seeing the inner workings like this." So we do some filming at the agency and Taylor and Eliza pick up their go-see information. And then we follow them to their appointments, both for print ads. Taylor gets a callback, but Eliza is still waiting. And she seems to be smoldering a bit. Something about her attitude reminds me of my best friend ... or my ex best friend. I'm not really sure anymore. But after our workday is done, I decide to give Mollie a call.

She doesn't answer and, as usual, I get her voicemail. "Hi, Mollie," I say as cheerfully as I can. "I hope you're over the flu now. I was just thinking of you and missing you and wanted to say hey. I'll be home by Wednesday and maybe we can get together. Later."

As I close my phone, I wonder if we really will get together. And if we do, will Mollie continue with her chilly jealousy act, or can we make an attempt to just be honest and talk about this?

Then I get what I think might be a good idea. Remembering Blake's invitation to go out on Valentine's Day, I wonder if we could go on a double date with Mollie and Tony — just like we used to do. So I call Blake and tell him about it.

"Let me guess ... you're worried that things will get too serious if it's just you and me alone, right?" he asks in a teasing tone.

I just laugh. "No, that's not it. I'm just feeling like Mollie and I are growing apart. And I don't want that. Besides, remember how much fun we used to have going out with them together? I miss that."

"Yeah, it does sound good. I'll call Tony and see what he thinks. And now, tell me, how was the slumber party?"

"Fortunately, it was a tiny bit more mature than middle school. Although one of the girls, Eliza Wilton, is kind of the jealous type. At first she seemed to set her sights on Paige, but I think she's mostly jealous of Taylor." Then I tell him about our plan to go to *Couture* tomorrow. "It sounds like Eliza wants to come too, but I think that's only going to make things worse. She's got this attitude — and it's weird because she's really pretty and her parents are like billionaires, but she's got this obsession with being a star, and I honestly don't think she's got the right stuff."

"Maybe she can buy her way to stardom."

"Maybe." We talk awhile longer and I suddenly realize

that I'm homesick. I miss Blake and Mollie and my mom. So I give Mom a call too, and she sounds like she misses us even more than we miss her.

"It's really given me a taste of empty nest syndrome," she admits. "And I'm not sure I like it."

"Well, it's not like we've moved out, Mom," I remind her.

"But it is just a matter of time … one day you will."

"Not any time soon."

"No, of course, there's no hurry. But I should tell you what I already told Paige."

"What?" Suddenly I'm alarmed. Surely Mom's not going to make us move out.

"Well … Jon and I … it's getting more serious. I just thought you should know, Erin."

"You're not running off to Vegas to get married, are you?"

She laughs. "Oh, it's not that serious. Not yet anyway. And definitely not to Vegas. We wouldn't do it like that."

"But you're actually thinking of marriage?" I feel stunned.

"It's hard not to *think* about it, Erin. Jon is a wonderful guy. And, for the first time since losing your dad, well, I feel happier than I ever thought possible."

I try to absorb this. My mom is falling in love?

"I don't want you to worry, honey. I just want you to be on the same page as Paige." She chuckles at her little play on words.

"Thanks … I appreciate it."

"And I know you'll be happy for me if Jon and I take our relationship to the next level."

"Sure." I try to sound convincing. "Of course."

But after I hang up I have this very bad feeling. It's not that I don't like Jon. Actually, I don't really know him that well, but what I do know of him, I like. I just feel like this is wrong. I can't imagine my mom being married to someone besides my dad. Yet, as much as I hate to admit this, I realize that I'm being very selfish. I suddenly realize that I'm no different than Eliza and how she acts about Taylor's success, or Mollie in the way she resents me doing *On the Runway*. And these are sobering thoughts. It's not easy to see yourself as you really are. So I decide the only thing I can really do about this Mom and Jon thing is to pray about it. And that is exactly what I do.

On Tuesday we all meet up at *Couture* magazine. As usual, I'm playing Camera Girl and enjoying hanging in the background as Paige and Taylor are given a tour of the magazine's headquarters and basically treated like rock stars. And although Eliza isn't completely ignored, I can tell that she's starting to feel like extra baggage. It doesn't help when JJ motions for her to move away so he can get a better shot of Taylor and Paige as they're chatting with the editor-in-chief.

They've even arranged for a mock photo shoot, just so we can include it in our show. But when they're done, the photographer seems pleased. "Some of these are so good that we might just use them anyway," he tells Taylor. "Great work, kiddo!"

As we're wrapping it up, Eliza leaves our group, saying she needs to use the restroom. But after awhile, we're getting ready to leave and she hasn't come back, so I offer to go check on her. To my surprise, she's still in the ladies' lounge — crying.

"Are you okay?" I ask.

She sniffs, then reaches for a tissue to blot her tears. "Do I look okay?"

I shrug.

"I'm just sick of this," she says as she tosses the wadded tissue into the trash. "I'm sick of being second-best, runner-up, second-fiddle ... the loser."

"You're hardly a loser," I tell her. "Good grief, do you know how many girls would love to be in your shoes?"

"I don't care about that."

"Then you know what?" I stare at her.

"What?"

"You might as well get used to it."

"Used to what?"

"Being a loser."

She blinks.

"Because as long as you look at life the way you're looking at it, you'll always be a loser."

"Are you going to talk about God again?"

"As a matter of fact, yes. Because the way I see it, Eliza, God has given you a whole lot. I mean, you are beautiful. And, other than your obsession with being first, you seem like you're intelligent. Plus you were born into money. You know how many girls would be happy to have just one part of that little formula? And yet you go on and on about what you don't have. Really, it's pathetic."

"Thanks a lot."

I would apologize for being so blunt, but a little dose of honesty might be just what she needs right now. "Eliza," I say more gently, "I'm just thinking that with all God has given you ... well, maybe he expects you to do something with it. Something more important than putting your face in front of a camera."

"Like what? Go feed starving kids in Africa?"

I nod. "Maybe. I think that could be a great beginning for you."

"And then what?"

"And then maybe God would show you what. But you need to quit focusing on yourself all the time, Eliza. It's not only shallow and selfish, it's totally unhealthy. And when you act like you've been acting, no one is going to want to be around you."

"Well, gee ... Thanks for the little pep talk."

"I guess I just call it as I see it."

She blows her nose then looks in the mirror. "Maybe it was a mistake to want to model."

"Well, we should probably go before they send out a search party."

She doesn't say another word about this conversation and I have no idea whether anything I said might do any good or make any difference, but I decide to put Eliza Wilton on my prayer list. And I think, in her own way, she's actually crying out for help.

On Wednesday morning we anxiously head for LaGuardia again and, thankfully, Paige makes it through security without any complications. And although we don't fly first class, Paige seems as happy as I am to be going home.

We're both totally surprised when we discover Mom, Jon, Blake, and Benjamin—along with balloons and a welcome home sign—waiting for us in baggage claim. JJ is even there to catch it on film.

After we gather up our luggage Jon offers to take us all out for dinner, but I play the spoiler. Whether it's because

I'm still feeling uneasy about him and Mom or because I'm just plain tired, I'm not sure. But I honestly do want to go to church tonight, and that's what I tell everyone when I make my apologies. Jon just smiles and says "another time." Then Mom takes my bags with her and Jon, and I go with Blake. Because we're crunching on time and because I'm starving, we decide to snag burgers at In-N-Out and eat them in the car before we head over to church.

Now we're sitting at church, and I can't even describe how good it feels to be in a worship service. It feels like it's been years since I've been here, and I can tell how much I need this. Still, I realize that I also need to be more supportive of my mom and her new boyfriend. I need to get over whatever it is that's making me resent Jon. During a quiet moment, I ask God to help me with that.

After church, Lionel comes over to say hello and inquires about New York. But I can tell he's curious about something else and I suspect he wonders why I'm here with Blake.

"How are your classes going?" I ask as a diversion.

"Really well. I'm finishing up a short documentary that turned out to be pretty good."

I make a face. "Okay, I won't ask you to go into details since I'd probably just get jealous. But I'm glad you're enjoying school."

"When do you think you'll come back?"

I consider this. "To be honest, I don't know. I'm committed to the show for the time being."

"And it's giving you some great hands-on experience," Blake injects.

Lionel eyes Blake, then nods. We talk a bit longer before we go our separate ways. And I can't help but feel something is amiss between Lionel and me. We used to be such good friends. As Blake drives me home, I try to wrap my head around the whole guy-girl thing, wondering why it's so tricky balancing out relationships with the opposite sex. Why can't you have it all?

"So we're still on for Valentine's Day?" Blake asks as he walks me up to our condo.

"I can't wait to shine up my bowling shoes," I tease.

He laughs. "Well, you might not need them after all."

"Oh, right ..."

"And Tony said *maybe* they would join us."

"Maybe?"

Blake shrugs. "If you think Mollie's been acting weird lately, I'm thinking it must be contagious because Tony seems different too."

"It's like we've offended them somehow," I tell him. "And I honestly can't remember doing anything that would've started this." I stifle a yawn as we get to my door. "I must still be on New York time, but thanks for taking me to church tonight. That was great."

He gives me a hug and a peck on the cheek, then takes off down the stairs like there's a fire somewhere. At first I wonder if he's embarrassed about the kiss ... but then I feel relieved that it was simply a peck. I don't think I'm ready for anything more just yet.

Mom's alone in the living room when I come inside. Just sitting on the couch with no lights on. "Are you okay?" I ask when I see her sitting there like a shadow.

"Just thinking."

I sit down next to her. "About what?"

"Your dad."

"Oh."

"You know, honey ... we didn't exactly have the greatest marriage."

This catches me off guard. "Huh?"

"Remember how we had our power struggles sometimes? He worked so many hours that I often resented it."

I nod. "Oh, yeah, I remember you guys would sometimes argue about housework."

She smiles. "Yes. I thought we should share the chores more."

"But why are you thinking about this?"

"I was just thinking that even though it wasn't a perfect marriage, even though we fought sometimes, I still miss it. I miss your dad immensely. But I miss having that relationship too."

"This is really about Jon, isn't it?"

She turns and looks at me. "I can tell it's bothering you, Erin."

I bite my lip.

"And that makes me question everything."

"Everything? You mean with Jon?"

She nods. "Yes. Maybe it is too soon."

"But Dad's been gone more than three years," I protest, knowing how incongruous this is to my previous emotions. Still, she's my mom—I want her to be happy.

"I know ..."

"And you and Jon seem to really like each other."

"Yes ... but ..." She studies me. "You seem to have a problem with it."

I wave my hand. "A little, I guess, but that's just me. You know what a stick-in-the mud I can be sometimes. I've never liked change."

Mom laughs. "Yes. I still remember when you threw a fit in fifth grade because I tossed your favorite sneakers even though you'd outgrown them."

"See," I tell her with a smile. "I'm just a little resistant to change."

"And you're resistant to Jon too." She sighs. "Even he could tell."

"I'm sorry."

"You can't help how you feel, Erin."

I consider this. Maybe I can't help how I feel, but I can control how I act. And, when it comes to Jon and Mom, I can tell I'm acting selfishly. "I know I've been a total brat about this, Mom. I mean, you obviously like Jon a lot. He obviously likes you. And I'm sure you know exactly what you're getting into. If you're really getting into something, that is."

She smiles. "Sometimes you just get a sense about someone—you know, early on—and you can tell that the relationship is special, like it's meant to be ... or at least it seems that way."

"And if that's how you feel about Jon, I am totally on board too."

"Really?" She looks hopeful.

"Really." I let out another yawn. "But now I need to call it a night. I'm exhausted."

"Yes, I can tell. I'm surprised Paige is still out. You girls had a long day and a long couple of weeks too. It felt like you were gone for months."

I nod and then I hug Mom. "I don't want you to be alone, Mom. And if you think Jon's the guy—then I'm happy for you."

As I go to bed, I think I really will be happy for her. Maybe not this very minute, but in time. Although I'm resistant to change, I eventually get with the program. Even those times when God has to give me a solid kick in the butt, I usually come along.

# *Chapter*
## 18

*"Look at us," Mom says as the three of us* stand in front of the mirror in Paige's bedroom on Valentine's Day. Paige has been playing stylist for Mom and me. And now all three of us are dressed and coiffed and ready for our dates.

Mom is wearing one of the outfits given to me when we visited the Dylan Marceau studio. It's a strawberry red two-piece suit with tasteful faux-fur trim around the collar and cuffs. "That suit is so perfect for you," I tell her. "You should just keep it."

Paige has on the light blue Rhiannon dress, which looks magical and will be perfect for the ballet performance that she talked Benjamin into taking her to see tonight. Her hair is twisted into a loose updo with tendrils of hair curling down her neck, and she has on dangly crystal earrings. "You look like a fairy princess," I tell her as she finishes up her makeup.

"And you look like a movie starlet from the old Hollywood glamour era," she tells me. But then she holds up the tube of red lipstick again. "Only you still need this."

"She's right," Mom tells me. "That dress is screaming for red lipstick."

So I comply and when I look in the mirror, I know they're probably right. I have on the same outfit I wore to the Dylan Marceau show and after party—the black and red Valentino. Valentino for Valentine's Day. Makes sense to me. And yet it's so not me. Or not the me I used to be. Even so, I must admit it's pretty cool. Who doesn't like to look glamorous some of the time?

I set up my camera to take some timed photos and we all strike poses and ham it up for several shots. "This is too fun," Mom says. But then the doorbell rings and it turns out to be Jon.

He compliments all of us on our outfits, but his eyes are fixed on Mom. And he looks slightly nervous, which surprises me because he's usually pretty cool and in control. But I think it's sweet that he's uneasy. Maybe he's trying to win our approval.

"Have fun," Paige calls out.

"And don't stay out too late," I tease.

Before long, Benjamin comes to pick up Paige. It's nice to see his face light up when he sees her and I can tell he's enchanted. "Have fun at the ballet," I call out as they leave. Benjamin makes a face then grins. "At least I'll be with the prettiest girl there."

Finally, Blake comes to the door and his expression is all I need to know that my outfit is working too. "Wow," he says as I reach for the red coat. "You look fantastic, Erin."

"Overdressed?"

He shakes his head. "Not at all."

"You're sure I don't need bowling shoes?"

He chuckles. "Well, that might be an interesting touch."

"Either way you look great," I tell him as I check out his suit. "This is kind of like prom, only better."

"Much better," he says.

"And Tony and Mollie are coming too?"

"Meeting us there."

But when we get to the restaurant and are seated at our table set for four, Mollie and Tony are nowhere in sight. We wait for about ten minutes, and we can tell our waiter is getting antsy. So Blake calls Tony and asks what's up. As Blake's smile fades into a frown, I can guess. They're not coming.

Blake closes his phone and shrugs. "Something came up."

"Oh." I try not to feel aggravated as the waiter clears away the now unnecessary place settings. "Why didn't they call earlier?"

"I don't know."

"Well, we won't let it ruin our evening, okay?" I force a smile for Blake's sake.

His eyes brighten. "No, we won't. In fact, I'm glad they didn't come tonight. Now I can have you all to myself."

So we end up having a very nice dinner — dinner for two. Afterward, we take in a movie, followed by ice cream. It's past midnight by the time he walks me to my door. He gives me one sweet kiss on the lips, thanks me for going out with him, and politely leaves. And I'm thinking this guy is smart — he's not pushing me, and just like reverse psychology it makes me want to take our relationship up a notch or two.

To my surprise, I'm the first one home. Not that I thought Paige would be home by now, but for some reason I thought Mom would be. I fully expected to come home and see her here — like that's what a mom is supposed to do. But instead of obsessing over her absence, simply because she's out with her boyfriend, I decide to get ready for bed. After all, Paige and I are grown up now. And Mom's an adult ... she can certainly stay out late if she likes.

But what if she doesn't come home at all tonight? No, I'm not going to retreat into my old fear — that of losing both parents. But what if she decided to spend the night at Jon's? In fact, how would I feel if she and Jon have already been spending nights together? With Paige and me off in New York all that time, it might've happened. While it might be juvenile, I find this possibility disturbing. Yet people do it all the time.

Then I replay what Mom told me the other day about how she and Jon are getting more serious. What did that actually mean? What if they decided to live together? How would I react to that? It's not easy being the only Christian in a family ... having different standards, values, convictions.

It's nearly one o'clock when I hear someone coming into the house. I tiptoe out to see that it's Mom. And she's alone. "You were out pretty late," I tell her as I go into the kitchen where she's pouring herself a glass of water.

"Oh, Erin." She smiles happily at me. "You'll never guess."

"Guess?" I shake my head. "What do you mean?"

Then she holds out her hand where I see a fairly large solitaire diamond glittering in the kitchen light. "Jon proposed."

"You're kidding." I just stare at the ring and try to wrap my head around this. Even though I'm unsure just how to feel, I wrap my arms around Mom and hug her. "Congratulations, Mom."

"I'm so happy!"

"I can see that."

"Is Paige home?"

"Not yet."

Mom looks down at her ring and slowly shakes her head as if she's still trying to take this in too. "I know it must seem like it all happened so quickly ..."

"Yeah, it does seem kind of fast."

"But when you know something's right ... and, well, Jon and I aren't getting any younger."

I laugh. "So that's why he looked so nervous earlier to-night. He had this all planned out."

"Valentine's Day," Mom sighs. "It was just perfect."

As she's telling me about where he took her and how he asked, Paige comes in and she has to start all over again. But it helps me to hear the story twice—I know it will take awhile before I can fully absorb what this means. Still, I do know that Jon is a great guy. And Mom is happy.

When I finally go to bed, I realize I *am* happy for Mom. How could I not be when she's so over the moon? Oh, sure, it does seem a little fast, but then Mom seems so confident that this is right. Why should I doubt her?

Even so, I feel troubled as I try to go to sleep, but it's not about Mom. Mollie has come to mind, and I decide that I'm going to pay her a visit tomorrow. Instead of calling and taking the chance she'll ignore me, I will go directly to her house. Since it's a Saturday she'll probably be home.

As I'm driving to Mollie's house on Saturday morning, I realize I need to adjust my attitude yet again. Instead of being angry at her, which I am, I need to be a friend to her. And to do this, I need to pray. I pray that God gives me the right words to say to her—not angry, judgmental words, but encouraging words. I want her to know how much I care about her ... how much I love her. To do that, I'll need God's help.

When I get to her house, her mom looks surprised to see me. "Erin, it's been awhile," she says as she lets me in. "The only time I see you anymore is on TV." She laughs like this is funny, but I can hear the jab in her tone and I suspect Mollie's attitude is infectious. "Mollie's still in bed," she says in a tired voice, "but maybe you can wake her up."

Of course, that's easier said than done. After I nudge her a couple times, Mollie opens her eyes and looks at me, then groans and rolls over. I almost wonder if she's been drinking. Is this a hangover?

"Come on, Mollie," I urge. "Time to get up."

"I'm tired."

"Talk to me now and you can sleep later," I persist. "Because I'm going to stay here and bug you until you get up."

Finally she sits up in her bed and looks at me with angry eyes. "What are you doing here?"

"I want to talk to you."

She shrugs. "So talk."

"Why did you and Tony bail on us last night?"

"We got in a fight."

"Oh." I nod. "I'm sorry. Are you guys okay?"

She nods back.

"But Mollie, I need to understand. Why are you treating me like I'm the enemy?" I ask. "Every time I call you, it seems like you either ignore my call, or you hang up, or you're just grumpy. What did I do to—"

"Maybe this isn't about *you*, Erin."

"Huh?"

"Why do you assume that everything is about you?"

"Well, I'm talking about our friendship. I have something to do with it. But maybe we're not friends anymore. Is that what you're trying to tell me?"

She looks down at her lap.

"And it would make me sad, but I could handle it, Mollie. I guess I just want to know why. Did I do something to hurt your feel—"

"There you go again . . . assuming this is about you."

Now I'm really frustrated. I mean, can she even hear herself? I take in a slow breath and try to keep from saying something harsh.

"No, Erin, you didn't do anything to hurt my feelings. Not specifically anyway. But you did kind of leave me behind."

"I left you behind?"

"We used to spend time together. Then you sort of abandoned me."

"But it feels like you abandoned our friendship," I reply. "I might've been busy with the show, but it's like you gave up completely. I mean, I've been trying to keep in touch as much as I could."

She looks at me with teary eyes now. And, for some reason, I suspect there's something else going on here—something Mollie's not telling me. But what?

"We grew apart, Erin. That's all."

"But I don't see how—"

"Fine." She grabs her pillow and clutches it to her stomach. "You want to know what's really wrong? I'll tell you." But then she doesn't say anything.

"What is it, Mollie?" I ask as gently as I can. "Talk to me."

"I'm pregnant."

*Wow.* This feels like it came from out of nowhere and I wonder if I heard her right. "What?" I say quietly.

"I'm pregnant." She looks evenly at me, waiting for me to say something.

I don't know what to say—how to respond. I want to ask her how this happened, but I already know that answer. And yet I also know that Mollie, like me, had made a commitment not to have sex before marriage. But obviously something had changed. "What are you going to do?"

She's running her hand over the pillow. "I'm going to have a baby."

"And then?"

"And then I'm going to be a mommy." But her voice is kind of flat and emotionless, as if she's not really feeling this. Or maybe she doesn't want to feel it. I'm just not sure.

"Oh."

"I know you're judging me, Erin."

"I'm not." I hold up my hands. "I'm just trying to grasp this. It's kind of shocking, you know."

"It hasn't been exactly easy for me. I could've used a best friend." She looks at me accusingly.

I consider this. For someone who could've used a best friend, she sure seemed to have been pushing me away. But I don't say this. "When is the baby due?"

"Mid-August." Her features soften a bit.

"Oh."

"And, yes, Tony is the dad."

"And he knows?"

"Oh, yeah."

"How's he dealing with it?"

"It depends."

"On?"

"On how he's feeling at the time. Sometimes he says we should just get married and be parents and that everything will be fine." She sighs.

"And other times?"

"Other times he thinks I should give the baby up for adoption."

"And what do you think?"

"I want to keep the baby." Her voice is full of determination now. "No matter what, I will keep the baby."

"Have you told your parents?"

She shakes her head no.

And then I hug her and she begins to cry quietly. "I'm still your friend," I assure her. "I *am* here for you. You're going to get through this, Mollie."

She wipes her tears on her pillow and nods.

"This isn't how I wanted my life to go," she says sadly.

"I know."

"But I just have to make the best of it. I have to be strong. For the sake of the baby, I have to keep it together."

"And you will."

I end up spending the entire day with Mollie, and there are moments when we're just doing normal things and I almost forget that she's pregnant. It's like we're just our same old selves. And then it hits me. *Mollie is going to have a baby.* Her life is changing in a huge way and it will never be the same. And I feel sad, like I'm grieving something that's being left behind. Maybe it's just childhood. Still, at the same time, I feel hopeful. I think Mollie will be a good mother. But I know it won't be easy, and I'm thankful I'm not in her shoes.

# *Chapter*

## 19

*The next two weeks aren't too busy for Paige* and me in regard to our show. We do a few fashion spots with a focus on swimsuits, beachwear, and vacation clothes. But mostly we're enjoying some down time, recovering from the New York trip, and gearing up for the Oscars red carpet. I'm also trying to spend more time with Mollie. I even went to the OB GYN with her. That wasn't exactly easy for me, and I felt irked that Tony was MIA right then. It's hard to tell what's going on with that boy, but Blake thinks he's mostly just really confused. Actually, both Tony and Mollie are. It's kind of like their lives—or their lives as they knew them—have been derailed.

Both Blake and I have been encouraging Mollie and Tony to plug themselves back into church. Mollie is getting more comfortable about being pregnant and finding that most of our friends are very understanding. And the ones who aren't—well, who cares?

But during these not-so-busy weeks, I notice that Paige is falling into something of a pattern. And it's got me worried.

She and Benjamin are going out a lot. I suspect it's partly to be seen and photographed because they're both publicity addicts. And it seems to make Helen Hudson happy each time Paige's face appears in some gossip rag. At least it used to please Helen. Today she sounds a little concerned.

"Hey, Jiminy Cricket," she says to me when she calls this morning. That's her nickname for me because she says I play Paige's "conscience," which is actually pretty ridiculous if you think about it — it's not like I can control Paige. "So how about that sister of yours?"

"What about her?" I ask.

"It looks like she and Benjamin have really been playing the club circuits lately. Do you think she's getting out of control?"

"Out of control?" I consider this. "You mean like drinking and partying too much?"

"Basically."

"I actually asked her about this last week," I confess. "I mean, about whether or not she's drinking. She assured me she's not into that anymore."

"What about Benjamin?"

"I didn't ask about him."

"Well, according to my sources, he's starting to get carried away again. You know he had a binge drinking problem on *Malibu Beach* the previous season. He allegedly cleaned up his act, but to be honest, I'm not so sure about the boy."

I want to ask her why she's telling me all this, except that I know why. She expects me to keep a watchful eye on my sister.

"It's not that I don't trust Paige," she says slowly. "But *On the Runway* is really starting to take off. The ratings are rising.

The sponsors are calling. And Paige is the main reason. That girl has the right stuff to make the show soar, Erin. In other words, I'm kind of like a mother hen here, and I have to protect my baby chicks, otherwise known as my assets."

"And you want me to protect my sister?"

"Well, I was thinking ... how about if you and your boyfriend went out with Benjamin and Paige? You kids would make a cute foursome and you could sort of keep an eye on things."

"I don't know if she and Benjamin will want us tagging along all the time." What I'm not saying is that I don't think Blake and I want to be stuck babysitting.

"Not all the time. Just some of the time. See what's really going on and make sure that your sister is safe. That's all I'm saying."

"I'll see what I can do."

"Thanks, Jiminy. You're really a great kid, you know that."

I laugh. "Yeah. I'm great at taking care of Paige, right?"

"A lot of people don't realize that stars need someone to ground them. It's like the old kite metaphor."

"The kite metaphor?"

"Yes. The star is like a kite—she needs to fly high and free, but she also needs someone on the ground holding onto the string."

"And that would be me?"

"You're a good kite flyer, Erin. And that's not so bad, is it?"

"I guess not."

So Blake and I end up inviting ourselves to meet up with Benjamin and Paige tonight. And although Blake was perfectly willing to hang with the stars—eager even—I feel guilty about keeping him out so late when he has classes in the morning.

Finally, we have to bow out, but I'm not feeling too worried because I could see that Paige wasn't drinking. And, as far as I could tell, Benjamin wasn't either.

"Do you think they were just on their best behavior because we were there?" Blake asks me as he's walking me to the door.

"That occurred to me."

"Does Helen Hudson really think you can control Paige?"

I laugh. "No. But I'm sure she's hoping." Then I thank him for coming along tonight, apologize for keeping him out so late, and we kiss and say good night. And although I'm still not sure it's wise taking our relationship to the next level, it's so nice. The butterflies are nice. Blake is just as attractive to me now as he was last year. Maybe even more so since we've both grown up a little. I just hope that I don't end up being sorry. Maybe I won't think about that.

Fortunately, the next few days are all about the Oscars and getting ready for the red carpet. This means that Paige has to try on a number of evening gowns and cocktail dresses, which we do with cameras running. Well, not running as she actually changes, but running as she models the different dresses by the various designers. It will be part of the show. It's like she does her own little runway segment of trying on outfits—trying to decide which one is perfect. She eventually settles on the Dylan Marceau gown, which he designed specifically for her. And I'm not sure if it's because she likes it the best—although I admit it looks awesome—or because she's still feeling slightly attracted to Dylan. It's a peacock blue satin in a slightly Asian style, fitted and classic with a long slit that reveals a fair amount of leg.

Despite Paige's begging me to wear a gown too, I insist on playing my role as Camera Girl on the red carpet this time. It's quite a battle, but to my relief, and after I remind her of our initial agreement, Fran finally agrees. "It's a nice contrast," she assures Paige. "And it adds interest."

When Oscar day comes, Paige and I head over to the Kodak Theater, where fans are already amassed and waiting. In contrast to when we did the Golden Globes, this time they seem to know who Paige is. They call out to her, whistling and cheering as she blows kisses and yells "thank you!" then bows. And, to my surprise, a few of them even call out to me.

We set up quickly, and it's not long before the first Academy Awards attendees begin trickling in. It's a little slow at first and, although Fran is there with the other pre-show producers, I feel worried that we're just not well known enough to get the really good traffic.

Then things pick up and I'm surprised at how many big-name celebs begin to come our way. But I'm not surprised at how they actually seem to enjoy chatting with Paige once they get here. As usual, she's in her element—the witty, charming young fashion expert. She smoothly transitions from one star to the next—from Amy Adams to Evan Rachel Wood. Even Mario Lopez stops by to say hi. And, really, it's a lot of fun. And too soon, it's over.

"Do you wish you could go inside?" I ask Paige as we're removing our mics and getting ready to leave.

"Of course." Then she smiles. "But Benjamin has invitations to some after parties and that will be almost as good."

"Sounds fun."

"Hey, maybe you and Blake could come along too."

Then I remind her that I already invited Mollie and Tony and Blake to watch the Oscars at our house with Mom and Jon. "But thanks anyway. Maybe another time."

By the time I get home, the Oscars are moving right along and Mom offers to reverse the show since it's recorded, but I assure her that I'm okay and use my laptop to catch up.

"How did the red carpet go?" Blake asks me as we're foraging for snacks during commercials.

"It seemed to go well," I tell him. Then I share some of the big names that Paige got to interview.

"Someday you girls will probably be on the real pre-show with the network," he tells me.

"I suppose that's possible," I admit. "I mean with Paige, who knows? But maybe I'll have moved on to something else by then."

He chuckles. "Yeah, like you'll be sitting in the awards ceremony as a nominee for cinematography."

"Wow, wouldn't that be amazing."

"It could happen."

The Oscars are about halfway done when I notice that Tony and Mollie have disappeared. But about fifteen minutes later, Mollie comes back inside and it's obvious that she's been crying.

"What's up?" I ask as I follow her to my room.

"We got in another fight," she says as she flops onto my bed. "Oh."

"Tony took off. Sorry he's being such a jerk."

"That's okay. I know he's got a lot on his mind. You both do."

"Maybe I can get a ride home with Blake."

"Or just spend the night here if you want."

She brightens. "Yeah. That'd be fun."

After the Oscars end and everyone goes home and Mom heads for bed, Mollie and I decide to stay up and watch late-night TV and eat more junk food. Just like we used to do back in high school. Then just as the *Tonight Show* is ending, there's a breaking news report. I'm about to turn it off, but something makes me stop.

"This just in—an automobile accident involving actor Benjamin Kross occurred around midnight on Laurel Canyon Boulevard. Emergency crews have responded and one fatality is reported. Laurel Canyon Boulevard will remain closed until the investigation and clean-up is completed—"

I grab onto Mollie's hand and our eyes lock. It feels like someone has just pulled out the earth from under me. "Paige," I whisper. "Paige is with Benjamin."

She just nods. I rush toward my mom's bedroom, shaking her awake and telling her what we just heard on the news. For a moment, we all just stand there in Mom's bedroom—too shocked to move. And then Mom is on the phone, talking to whoever's at Channel Five and trying to gather the facts. But as she listens, I can see the color draining from her face. And then she hangs up and reaches for me, pulling me to her as she sobs. "The fatality was a woman," she gasps. "She hasn't been identified yet, but—"

And the three of us huddle together, sobbing and clinging to each other. I am aching in a way that is even harder and deeper than when my dad died. How is this possible? How could this happen again? Why didn't I go with Paige when she asked me tonight? Why didn't I do something to prevent this? I wish it were me, not Paige. How can this be?

# Chapter
## 20

*"What's going on?"*

I turn to see Paige coming into Mom's room. And, for a moment, I think I'm delusional. "*Paige?*" I cry. Then we all rush at her and hug her and look at her and then cry some more.

"You're okay!" I say finally. "You're alive!"

"Of course I'm alive. What's this about anyway?"

"Oh, Paige," Mom sobs. "We were so frightened."

"What is it?" Paige demands. "What's happened?"

Now we step back and I turn to Mom, hoping she can explain.

"There's been a car wreck," Mom says soberly.

"A car wreck?" Paige looks confused. "Who?"

"Benjamin."

Paige's hand flies to her mouth. "Benjamin? Is he okay?"

"I'm not sure. There was one fatality ... a woman ... we assumed it was you."

"You were supposed to be with him," I remind her. "We really thought it was you."

Paige sinks to the chair by Mom's bed, cradling her head in her hands.

"Why weren't you with him?" Mom asks.

Paige looks up with tear-filled eyes. "Ben was drinking and he wanted to go to another party. But I wanted to come home. And I wanted to drive. We argued and he walked out on me. I called for a cab, which took forever, and now—now this?"

"I wonder who was with him," I say, and then regret it.

"A woman?" Paige just shakes her head. "Who knows who it could be?" She reaches for her phone, but then freezes and just stares blankly at it. "I don't even know who to call. How can I find out how he is, Mom?"

"Let me handle this," Mom says. Then she's on the phone again. She gets the name of the hospital, and offers to drive Paige there.

"You can go too if you want," Mollie tells me.

"That's okay," I say. "I think they can handle this without me."

"Want us to call and let you know?" Mom asks as they're leaving.

"Yeah—thanks. I'm pretty certain I won't be sleeping anyway."

So Mollie and I remain behind, and we decide to pray. We pray for Benjamin and for the family of whoever was riding with him tonight. And, although I'm exceedingly thankful it wasn't my sister, I can't help but feel connected to this woman too. Eventually Mollie goes to sleep, but I continue to pace and pray, asking God to have mercy on Benjamin.

The ringing of the phone makes me jump, jerking me back to reality. It's now nearly four in the morning, and Mom's voice is on the other end. "Benjamin is in fair condition," she tells me. "He's unconscious due to a head injury, and he has some broken bones."

"Oh."

"And the woman passenger—" Mom's voice breaks. "She was Mia Renwick."

"Mia?" I try to wrap my mind around this. "Mia Renwick is dead?"

"Yes."

"Oh no ..." I'm stunned. "How's Paige?"

"She's holding up on the exterior, but I can tell she's hurting on the inside. Right now she's with Benjamin's mom, trying to comfort her."

"What about Mia's mom?"

"It's very sad, Erin. Very, very sad. My heart aches for her family. They're beside themselves. And it doesn't help that the media is here. Not that I blame them, this is big news. And already people are speculating about criminal charges or wrongful death suits against Benjamin. It's bad and going to get worse."

"Poor Paige."

"Yes. But I'm so thankful, Erin. So thankful."

"Me too, Mom."

"Anyway, I thought you'd want to know."

"Tell Paige I'm praying for Benjamin ... and her too."

"Thanks, honey, I'm sure she'll appreciate that. I know I do."

Then we say "I love you" and hang up.


The next couple of days pass in a blur. I commit myself to remain by Paige's side, trying to absorb some of the shockwaves as I walk with her through this mess. The media seems to be everywhere, and although Helen Hudson and our crew are relieved that Paige is safe, they're also very concerned about how this will reflect on our show. I'm not really sure that I care. Right now, the success of our show seems very small compared to the tragedy around us.

We can hardly get in or out of the hospital without an assault of media and paparazzi. Paige is asked to tell her story again and again, which she does honestly and graciously. And when she's asked why she wasn't the one in the car with Benjamin, she tells the truth. With no candy coating or spin-doctoring, she says that Benjamin had been drinking and that she wanted to drive him home. "He refused to give me his keys, and I refused to get in the car with him."

"Lucky for you," the journalist says.

"But not so lucky for Mia," Paige says sadly.

Then when the reporters ask why Mia was with Benjamin, Paige simply states that she doesn't know.

But one pushy reporter keeps pushing. "Come on," he urges her, "you must have some idea."

"Mia was at the same party," she patiently explains. "And we even talked to her briefly."

"So you were on friendly terms with Mia?"

"We weren't really good friends, but we weren't enemies either."

"Do you think Benjamin and Mia were getting back together?" the reporter persists. "Is that why she was in the car with him?"

"That's a question that only Benjamin can answer," Paige says. "And that's not what matters right now. We need to keep Benjamin, as well as Mia's family, in our thoughts." *And in our prayers*, I think.

Three days after the wreck, Benjamin regained consciousness, but his memory of that night was still foggy. He actually thought it was Paige who was with him and was shocked to learn it was Mia — and even more shocked to learn she is dead. But today, it seems Benjamin's memory returned completely.

"He's really depressed tonight," Paige tells me as I drive her home from the hospital.

"Not surprising."

"He's blaming himself."

"Well, he should."

"Yes, but there's a little more to the story."

"Oh?"

"Benjamin knows he shouldn't have been driving," she tells me. "And it wasn't his idea to give Mia a ride. It seems she kind of invited herself. And she'd been drinking too."

"Really?"

"Yes. And apparently she started a fight with him while they were driving and that fight was what caused the wreck. Well, that combined with the fact that he was impaired. He doesn't deny that."

"It might be something he'll have to prove in court," I tell her.

"His attorney is already insisting on blood alcohol level reports."

I just shake my head. What a mess. It's something that could've been avoided. Should've been avoided. But what point is there in saying this now? Besides, it's not Paige's fault. I know she's learned some hard lessons from all this.

"How do you feel about Benjamin?" I ask her as we're going up to our condo unit.

"The truth?"

"Yeah. I mean this is me, your sister."

She nods. "I know. Well, I was ready to break up with him that night. I mean, I practically said as much. But to break up now, when he's like this? Well, it's a little harsh, don't you think?"

And I guess she's making the right choice here. I mean, it might be cruel to dump Benjamin when he's down like this, although I can tell it's taking a toll on Paige too. But then, I remind myself, God sometimes uses hard things like this to get through to us. And Paige admits to me that she has been praying lately.

"I'm sure I don't pray as much as you do. And I might not even be doing it right," she tells me.

"I don't know that there's a right or wrong way," I assure her. "I think it's mostly just that you talk to God."

"Well, I'm trying. And it even feels like God is listening. When I get done, I always feel better. In fact, I told Benjamin that he should try it."

"Really? What did he say?"

"He said he's thinking about it. But it's a pretty new concept to him. I mean, he's never gone to church at all."

"Hey, maybe Blake could visit him," I suggest. "They seem to get along okay. And Blake's got a solid and strong faith that might encourage Benjamin."

The next morning, Paige runs it past Benjamin, and he's okay with it too. Blake went to visit him and called me afterward.

"It's going really well," Blake tells me. "Benjamin is really open to hearing about God. I gave him a Bible and a book about the basics of Christianity. And he was cool with it."

One week after the car wreck, a memorial service is held for Mia Renwick. I go with Paige and we sit with Benjamin and his family. I feel a little uneasy about this, but Paige assures me that it's the right thing to do. And when Benjamin leans over, quietly crying, I notice his bruised and cut face, as well as his arm in a cast, and I feel some sympathy for him. But mostly I feel for Mia's family. And the service seems sad and sort of hopeless to me. I can't imagine how her parents are feeling right now. And, as I pray for them, I remind myself that God's mercy is far bigger than I can even imagine.

Two weeks have passed since the wreck, and Paige seems to be more like her old self, which is a good thing since we're now planning our Paris trip. We're at the studio, meeting with Helen and the others. I'm thinking that this might be just what we need, or rather what Paige needs. Something to distract her from Benjamin and his troubles, which seem to be piling higher daily.

"We're structuring this trip a bit differently than New York," Fran is telling us. "Each show will feature one French designer for an entire episode, so we really have to make these interviews count. And we'll only do one or two actual fashion shows."

"That sounds good." Paige's eyes light up with interest. "I like doing the interviews."

"Great." Fran nods. "We'll also try to set something up with *Vogue Paris* and whatever else Leah gets lined up for us by then."

"That all sounds fun." Paige nods eagerly.

"And, sad as it is," Helen says, "all this publicity with

Benjamin and Mia has sparked even more interest in our show internationally as well as closer to home." She frowns. "How is Benjamin these days, anyway?"

Paige gives a quick report about his health—other than a broken arm and some cracked ribs, he's pretty much back to normal. "He's taking a very serious look at life though," she tells them. "And he's spending a lot of time with his attorney."

"I can imagine." Helen shakes her head. "And we don't want to tell you how to live your life, Paige, but we would like to encourage you to distance yourself from him a bit."

"Paris will be handy for that," Fran says lightly.

"I'm okay with distancing myself," Paige tells them. "In fact, that's what I've been trying to do."

Helen just nods then glances at her notes. "While we're on the subject of men and romance, there is a rumor circulating in the fashion world that a certain designer might be making designs on you, Paige."

"What?" Paige looks puzzled. "Who?"

"Dylan Marceau."

"Oh." Paige actually looks slightly embarrassed. "*Really?*"

Helen laughs. "Well, you know how rumors can be. But we thought that, if you were on board with this, we'd like for you to spend some time with Dylan in France. He'll be doing a show during that same time. And perhaps he could sort of show you around. You know he grew up there. What do you think?"

Paige's eyes light up now. "Seriously? That would be fantastic!"

Helen looks relieved. "Okay, Fran, see what you can set up."

As we leave the studio, Paige is starting to bubble over. "Can you believe it, Erin? Paris and Dylan Marceau," she says happily. "Does it get any better than that?" And suddenly she's gushing about what she thinks is about to become the biggest trend in fashion and how Paris is the fashion capital of the world. That's when I realize that my sister's kite is starting to soar again. And this time, I will do all that I can to hold onto the string. I can't control my sister or her choices, but I can try to be a good influence. And, even more than that, I can pray.

As we're walking to the car, her optimism begins pulling me in. I realize that her enthusiasm is contagious. Before long, I'm just as happy as she is and we both begin practicing our rusty French, although hers is much better than mine. And I think, okay, this is going to be fun.

"Vive la France!" she shouts when we get to her car.

"Vive la vie!" I shout back.

Then Paige hugs me. "Yes," she says, "Hurrah for life!"

"Amen!"

# DISCUSSION QUESTIONS FOR

## CATWALK

1. Early in the story, Erin expresses an interest in green fashion. What are your thoughts on this kind of clothing? What do you think of Paige's opinion of green fashion?

2. Paige sometimes seems to live for fashion. Do you think that's a good thing? Why or why not?

3. What's your reaction when Paige and Benjamin appear to be getting back together? What would you advise Paige to do?

4. Why do you think Erin has such a problem with judging Benjamin? Explain how you'd deal with a situation like that.

5. Were you surprised when Paige got into so much trouble with the security guards at the airport? How do you think a situation like that should be handled? What could Paige have done differently?

6. Erin seems to vacillate between criticizing her sister and running to her rescue. Why do you think that is? What do you think Erin could do differently?

7. Paige sometimes seems to suffer from princess syndrome. Why or why not might this be a problem?

8. On a scale of one to ten, how do you rate as a princess? (1 = I'd rather scrub toilets than be seen as or treated like a princess. 10 = I was born to be treated like royalty.) Explain why you feel this way and what being a princess means to you.

9. What's your reaction when Paige helps Erin to improve her fashion image? How would you react if you were Erin?

10. Who did you most relate to when the girls have their "slumber party": Erin, Paige, Eliza, or Taylor? Describe why.

11. What was your reaction when you read about Benjamin's car wreck? (Concern, outrage, sadness, criticism, or something else?) What made you feel this way?

12. Do you think Paige should continue her relationship with Benjamin or end it? Why?

ON THE RUNWAY

# RENDEZVOUS

A Novel

Bestselling Author
## Melody
## Carlson

# Chapter
## 1

"*Not another French movie,*" *I complain* when I see Paige setting a new DVD on the counter. "We don't want to OD on Paris before we even get there."

"This movie happens to be for Mom. She mentioned that *To Catch a Thief* is one of her favorites, and since she doesn't get to go with us, I thought we could at least humor her a bit." Paige proudly holds up what I'm guessing is a new handbag. "And this, little sister, is a gift from *Hermès, Paris.*"

"A gift or a bribe?" I question as I study the square leather purse with a silver clasp. If it wasn't pink, I might actually like it.

"Let's call it an *enticement*." She makes a sly grin. "Not that I needed any, since I already wanted to visit Hermès. They're at the top of my list. I absolutely adore Hermès."

"You and Paris Hilton—maybe you were twins separated at birth," I tease. I know the Paris Hilton connection drives Paige nuts. Especially since some celeb-trackers have compared Paige to the hotel heiress, which I personally think is rather insulting to my sister. In my opinion, Paige has more class than Paris. Not that I would ever admit that to anyone.

"For your information, Paris Hilton wasn't the first celebrity to discover Hermès." Paige opens the pink bag, retrieving a black and white scarf, which I assume is also Hermès. "In fact, Jackie O and Grace Kelly were both fans of Hermès decades ago. Hence the *Kelly bag*."

"Kelly bag?"

She holds up her bag and gives me a *duh* expression. "*The Kelly bag*. Designed for Grace Kelly back in the forties, I think. Anyway, it was a long time ago." Paige gets a faraway look. "What I *really* want is the Birkin bag."

"Birkin bag?" I ask, at the risk of a long fashion lecture.

"Jane Birkin, the actress, you know."

"Right." I nod. Of course I know who Jane Birkin is. I *was* in film school back in BS. BS is not what it sounds like — it's actually my new personal shorthand code for Before (the) Show. Anyway, I do know that Jane Birkin was in films during the sixties and later, and I also know she was a fashionista too. Sort of like Audrey Hepburn, but not nearly as popular. "So Jane Birkin has an Hermès bag named after her too?"

"Only the most popular, most expensive, and hardest to get handbag of all time." She shakes her head sadly. "The waiting list is, like, years."

"Even for you" Paige gives me a slightly catty smile. "I suppose we'll find that out in Paris next week."

"Maybe you'll totally wow Monsieur Hermès and he'll design a special *Paige bag* just for you."

She laughs. "For starters, there is no Monsieur Hermès. Not as in a designer like Calvin Klein or Ralph Lauren. Hermès was originally a family-owned leather company. They made saddles in the 1800s."

"From horses to handbags," I say with irony. "Fashion is so fickle."

Paige places a finger under her chin as if thinking. "Come to think of it, there is a Monsieur Damas-Hermès, but I don't think he's a designer per se. He just runs the company. And he's one of the richest men in the world."

"Will we meet him?" I'm not sure I even care, since I'm not that into money, but it might be interesting.

"I doubt it." She picks up the DVD. "So anyway, back to tonight's plans ... I thought we'd do something special for Mom, since it's only three days until we leave for Paris, and I could tell she was feeling bummed last night when we watched *An American in Paris*."

"I thought it was because Grandpa had always been a Leslie Caron fan."

"That's what she wanted us to think," Paige replies. "Really, she wishes she could go with us. She even tried to get time off from Channel Five, but there's no way."

"Too bad she didn't take Helen Hudson up on the offer to help produce the show back when she had the chance last December."

Paige shakes her head. "No way. I would not want Mom producing for us. I love her, but I don't want to work for her. Besides, she's as fashion-challenged as you are."

"Thanks a lot." I make a face at her.

"At least you're learning, Erin. Not that Mom couldn't catch on, but she loves her news job. And what about Fran? She totally gets the show. Can you imagine Mom and Fran working together?"

I nod, knowing that she's right. "So what are you going to do that's so special tonight? I mean, besides the movie."

"I ordered dinner from Patina and I thought we'd set a really pretty table and do candles and flowers — the works.

Then we can watch *To Catch a Thief*." She frowns. "Although I'd rather watch *Funny Face* again. That's such a great Paris movie."

"You mean because it's all about fashion?"

She sighs. "Fashion and Paris and Audrey Hepburn ... it doesn't get much better, does it?"

I chuckle. "Well, I'll admit that I did like *Funny Face*, but that had more to do with the photography focus and Fred Astaire's dancing skills. Plus the fact that Audrey's character was more into philosophy than fashion. I could appreciate her reluctance to become a model."

Paige points her finger at me. "Come to think of it, her character was a lot like you."

"As a matter of fact she was, at least in the first part of the movie. I could sort of relate to her."

"And you know ..." Paige squints at me as she makes a frame with her thumbs and forefingers. "You even kind of look like her."

"Oh, yeah, sure." I shake my head.

"Seriously, Erin, you really do. You're both petite and you both have that pixie sort of face, big expressive eyes, dark hair."

Now I just laugh. "Okay," I say cautiously, "what do you want from me?"

She makes a face. "I'm serious, Erin. You are an Audrey type. I can't believe I never noticed it before. That explains why you look so great in those little black dresses." She frowns. "But maybe we should change your hair. Then you'd really look like her."

"I don't think so."

She takes my chin in her hand, tilting it up. "Really, I'm surprised I didn't see it before, Erin."

"Well, thanks," I say quickly. "I think. But you have to admit that I'm not nearly as skinny as Audrey was. Do you think she was anorexic?"

Paige considers this. "I don't really know for sure, although she nearly starved during World War two and that probably took its toll. I've always adored Audrey Hepburn, and she was and is the most fashionable woman ever, and every single thing she wore instantly became *haute couture*. That might not have happened if she hadn't been so thin."

"And see—" I point my finger at her. "That's one thing about fashion that makes me want to scream and pull my hair out. *Stick-thin models*. Seriously, if we interview any stick girls in Paris, I might not be able to control myself from asking them about their health and eating habits." I kind of chuckle. "Or maybe I'll just bring in a bunch of croissants and pastries and sit there and noisily pig out in front of them."

Paige presses her lips together with a slightly creased brow. "You know, Erin, that's an interesting angle. The skinny trend had really been changing a couple years ago. Several designers even banned overly thin models from their runways. Now that I think about it, though, it seems like some of them went back to their old ways. Especially internationally. You know, maybe we should do a show that specifically addresses this issue."

"Seriously?"

She nods eagerly as she picks up her cell phone. "I'm going to call Fran right now and see what she thinks."

"What about dinner? Is there something I can do?"

"You could run and get some flowers. Something Parisian-looking, like you picked it up from a street vendor, okay?"

"What about Jon?" I ask. Jon and Mom have been engaged for a couple of months, but already he feels like family.

"Don't worry. I already invited him. He even offered to pick up dinner on his way over. We're aiming to eat at eight. Is that okay?" She's got the phone to her ear now.

"Sure."

As Paige begins explaining to Fran about my anorexic models story idea, even giving me credit for thinking of this angle, I grab my bag and head down to my Jeep, trying to remember where the closest florist shop is located. The only one I can think of is a few miles down the freeway and it's commuter traffic time now. Still, it's the least I can do, considering Paige has already put this Parisian dinner plan together for Mom. I'm impressed that she cared enough to go to this trouble. My sister used to be a lot more self-centered and selfish. But I can tell she's changing. And that's pretty cool.

It hasn't always been easy being Paige Forrester's little sister. It's even harder playing Camera Girl, Fashion Flop, or even Jiminy Cricket, as our producer, Helen Hudson, likes to call me, since a big part of my job is keeping Paige out of trouble. But sometimes it can be kind of fun, and I am actually looking forward to Paris.

Yet, at the same time, I wonder just how needed I'll be on our reality show now. Because, to everyone's surprise, Paige has really grown up a lot in the past couple months. She's taking life more seriously, taking responsibility for more things both at work and at home, and actually thinking about others. I realize it's greatly due to Mia Renwick's tragic death on Oscar night. Talk about a tough wake-up call for everyone. For a few horrid hours, we actually thought it was Paige who'd been killed in the car wreck. That's a night I never want to relive.

Paige had gone to a party with Benjamin after the Oscars, but when they were leaving and she found out he'd been drinking, she refused to ride with him and called a cab. Then Mia made the fatal mistake of getting into Benjamin's car. Now Benjamin has been charged with vehicular homicide but, according to Benjamin, both he and Mia had been drinking. He claims Mia actually caused the accident when she lost her temper and physically laid into him while he was driving in the Hollywood hills, even grabbing and twisting the wheel right before the accident occurred. Benjamin says that Mia was still enraged over their breakup several weeks earlier. Apparently the evidence is starting to support Benjamin's side of the story too, because witnesses reported Mia was acting hostile when she and Ben left together, and her blood-alcohol level in the toxicology reports was very high. Ben's blood alcohol, however, was under the legal limit when the police arrived and administered the Breathalyzer. Also, according to Paige, the police said the skid marks at the scene of the accident match his story—it appears someone changed the direction of the vehicle very suddenly.

Even so, I still think Benjamin's guilty. I realize I'm probably more judgmental than most when it comes to drinking and driving, but I think anyone who gets behind the wheel after consuming alcohol should be locked up for a while. Really, what could it hurt?

And I'm not sorry that Paige is keeping her distance from Benjamin now. Oh, she talks to him on the phone sometimes. I call them mercy chats. Mostly she's worried that he's feeling depressed. Hey, he should be depressed. A young woman is dead because of him. He can claim it's Mia's fault, but he was the one driving that night. It's not like I hate him or anything. I really don't. In fact, I pray for him every day. I just don't think he should get off too easily. That's all I'm saying.

Thinking all this, and because I'm stuck in traffic that's not budging an inch, I decide to give Blake a quick call, since I know he met with Benjamin this morning. They've actually been doing a Bible study together. I'm not sure if Benjamin is taking it seriously or just hopes that it will improve his bad boy image, but it sure won't hurt him to hear some truth either.

"Old Ben was pretty bummed today," Blake tells me. "Mia's parents have launched what feels like a full-blown smear campaign. They're talking to publicists and any press that will listen, trying to make Benjamin out to be a murderer who's about to get off scot-free."

"That's not so far from the truth."

"But Erin, they're even comparing him to OJ Simpson. It's like they want him ruined forever. It might even crush his movie deal."

I feel my fingers tightening on the steering wheel, which is pointless since the car isn't even moving. I let go and take in a deep breath. "Okay, I'll admit the OJ thing seems harsh. But it's true that some celebrities beat the rap simply because of their names. It irks me when I see one going off on his merry way like, no big deal. That's just not fair. Maybe losing the movie deal is for the best."

"What about what Jesus said about not throwing stones?" he asks me.

I consider this. "Yeah, I know ... and you're right. But I still think Benjamin should assume some blame for—"

"He knows that he's partly to blame and he wants to admit it. But his attorney is counseling him to continue proclaiming his innocence."

"See, and that bugs me. Maybe if Benjamin took some responsibility for the accident, Mia's parents would let up on him."

"Maybe ..." Blake sounds discouraged.

"I'm sorry, Blake, I don't mean to get on my soapbox. Sorry I sound so negative. I know it's not fair for me to take it out on poor Ben. I really do feel sorry for him and it's cool that you're spending time with him." I peer down the freeway with four lanes of immobile traffic as far as I can see. "It doesn't help that I'm stuck on I–5, and you know how aggravated I get. Patience is not my strong suit."

"Where you headed anyway?"

"I was supposed to pick up some flowers for my mom. Paige is giving her an authentic Parisian dinner tonight."

He laughs. "To make up for leaving her home?"

"Yeah, and we have to watch *To Catch a Thief* with her too, since it's a film that's set on the Mediterranean."

"Man, how many French movies have you girls watched already?"

"Too many." To pass the time, I actually start to list the films. "I really liked *Amelie*," I admit. "And *La Vie en Rose* was amazing, but it was kind of a downer too. Paige's all-time favorite is still *Funny Face*. And any other film with her favorite fashion icon—Ms. Hepburn. We watched *Charade* and even *Sabrina*, which is only partially set in Paris." I notice some of the brake lights flashing and I realize that cars are starting to move. "I better hang up," I say quickly. "Thanks for keeping me company in the traffic jam. Please don't take what I said about Benjamin too seriously. I really do care about him."

"I know you do. And if it's any comfort, I agree with a lot of what you said. But Benjamin needs friends more than accusers right now."

"I'll keep that in mind." I say good-bye and hang up as I put the Jeep into gear. After snarking and going on about

DUIs, I'm fully aware that driving while talking or texting on the phone or while doing a lot of other distracting things, like eating, is just as dangerous as driving while intoxicated. After all, I've given Paige that same lecture more than once when I've caught her putting on mascara or lip gloss while she's driving. Although I'll admit I haven't noticed her doing it lately.

Once again I'm reminded that my role on our show might be more expendable than I realized. It might be written out even sooner than I expected. Perhaps it's right around the corner. Because I'm fully aware that *On the Runway* does not need Camera Girl to make it a success—Paige Forrester is what makes the show so popular. Sometimes, like right now, I worry that I'm just an unnecessary distraction. Extra baggage. Another expense. Really, the show would be perfectly fine without me.

And here's what's really weird, especially when I remember how much I whined about being hijacked into reality TV back in the beginning. The truth is that *I would not be perfectly fine without the show*. I really like being part of it. I'm actually learning a lot about film and production—much more than I ever would've learned by now in film classes. And I love being with Paige. I don't even mind being called Camera Girl or even Jiminy Cricket that much. What I do mind is not being needed anymore. That seriously worries me.

## On the Runway Series
## from Melody Carlson

When Paige and Erin Forrester are offered their own TV show, sisterly bonds are tested as the girls learn that it takes two to keep their once-in-a-lifetime project afloat.

**Premiere**
Book One

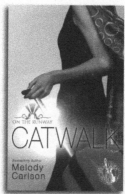

**Catwalk**
Book Two

**Rendezvous**
Book Three

**Spotlight**
Book Four

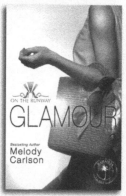

**Glamour**
Book Five

**Ciao**
Book Six

*Available in stores and online!*

**ZONDERVAN®**
.com

# Carter House Girls Series
## from Melody Carlson

Mix six teenage girls and one '60s fashion icon (retired, of course) in an old Victorian-era boarding home. Add boys and dating, a little high school angst, and throw in a Kate Spade bag or two ... and you've got the Carter House Girls, Melody Carlson's new chick lit series for young adults!

**Mixed Bags**
Book One

**Stealing Bradford**
Book Two

**Homecoming Queen**
Book Three

**Viva Vermont!**
Book Four

**Lost in Las Vegas**
Book Five

**New York Debut**
Book Six

**Spring Breakdown**
Book Seven

**Last Dance**
Book Eight

*Available in stores and online!*

**ZONDERVAN®**
.com

Want FREE books?
FIRST LOOKS at the best new teen reads?
Awesome EXCLUSIVE video trailers,
contests, prizes, and more?

We want to hear from YOU!

Give us your opinion on titles, covers, and stories.
Join the Z Street Team today!

Visit ZStreetTeam.Zondervan.com to sign up

Connect with us:

 /GoodTeenReads         @GoodTeenReads

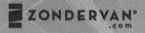